Involuntary Turnover

A Kat Voyzey Mystery, Book 1

Cheri Baker

Published by Adventurous Ink, Seattle

This is a work of fiction. Names, characters, places, and incidents either are the product of the author's imagination or are used fictitiously. Any resemblance to actual persons, living or dead, events, or locales is entirely coincidental.

First edition. December 7, 2013.

978-0-9910811-0-3

Copyright © 2013 Cheri Baker

All rights reserved. Published in the United States by Adventurous Ink. No part of this book may be reproduced or transmitted in any form or by any means, electronic or mechanical, including photocopying, recording, or by any information storage and retrieval system, without written permission from the publisher.

Book design by Patrick Baker
Cover art by The Book Brander

For my friends in HR.

CHAPTER ONE

THE LAST DAY IN OCTOBER began with a violation of the employee dress code and ended with a dead employee in the medical records department. I've always said I like my job because of the variety, but this was a bit much, even for me.

My name is Kat Voyzey, and for the last three years, I've been the human resources director at Holy Heart Medical Center. Our hospital is the oldest and most famous in Seattle, having been founded by pioneering nuns after the Great Fire of 1889 burned the entire city to the ground.

Most human resources people have a specialty, and mine is employee relations. That's a fancy way of saying I deal with all the drama that crops up in the workplace.

When interns get caught making out in an exam room, I get the call. When a bipolar medical assistant goes off her meds and throws a tray full of food at her coworker, I get the call. And when a heart surgeon making three hundred thousand dollars a year is too afraid to tell his receptionist she smells like unwashed livestock... Well, you get the idea. With over two thousand employees in the mix, there's always a crisis somewhere.

That's why I wasn't surprised when Claire Sutcliffe was sitting in my office when I arrived at work. Every new day brought fresh problems to my door, usually in the form of someone being annoyed with someone else.

"My manager is insane," she said.

"Good morning to you too."

"Seriously, she's lost her mind. We should get her tested."

As I hung up my wet jacket, I wished that for just this once, Halloween at the office wouldn't be a total shit-show.

I sat down next to Claire and asked her what happened.

She rolled her eyes. "Shannon says I have to go home and change out of my costume. I live ninety minutes away, and it's the middle of rush hour. I won't get back until after lunch! She's being is ridiculous."

I considered Claire's costume. She had wrapped her narrow frame with white cotton batting, giving her the appearance of a cottony cylinder. Her short black hair was confined in a white knit cap.

"What are you, a cotton ball?"

"Um. Not exactly." She stood and gestured to the ground beneath her feet where a thin white cord dangled.

My eyebrows must have hit my hairline. Claire smirked at me, her expression triumphant. Her joke had hit the mark.

"You're a tampon!"

"Yup. Funny, eh?" Claire laughed, and I couldn't help but crack a smile. This was inventive!

"And what do you want from me?" I asked, leaning back in my chair. "Shannon's within her rights to send you home. Your costume is funny, but you'll offend as many people as you amuse."

I was already imagining the fallout. One of our elderly patients would emerge from the restroom and see a giant tampon walking toward them. Then they'd fall down and break a hip. Later would come the lawsuit for emotional distress. And the news stories. Then, finally, the made-for-TV movie: *"When Tampons Attack: How Seattle's Top Hospital Fell from Grace."*

Claire sighed. "I know. But I really don't want to miss half a day's pay for this. Any ideas?" She pulled the knit hat off and smoothed her dark hair with one hand. That got me thinking.

"How about this," I thought out loud. "Lose the rope and the hat. Fold up that batting so it's shorter and wider. You can be a cotton ball or a cloud. That might fly."

Claire reached down between her knees and with some energetic tugging removed the rope. After careful re-wrapping, aided by my office stapler, her costume seemed sufficiently toned down.

She stood in front of my office mirror and turned from side to side before giving me an approving nod.

"Thanks. I figured you'd know what to do."

"You're welcome. And don't be too hard on Shannon. You know she can get in trouble for what you wear. I know it sounds silly, but that's the way it goes when you're the boss."

"Yeah, I know," she said. "But I wish we could have more fun around here."

Me too, I thought.

"One more thing," I said as she turned to leave. "Go ask Shannon if you can stay at work and be a cloud. She'll probably be cool about it, but you won't win any points by telling her you second guessed her and came to me."

Claire departed, leaving my office door open behind her. I gingerly picked up the white cord she left behind and dropped it in my trash can.

I considered the matter successfully resolved. At the end of the day, keeping the boss happy is a good career move.

CHAPTER TWO

I HEARD THE FAMILIAR JINGLE of keys as Jocelyn arrived and unlocked the metal filing cabinets that house our personnel files.

"Good morning, Jocelyn," I called out.

"Morning, Kat!"

The overhead lights buzzed faintly as she flipped switches and brought the department to life. A few moments later she swept into my office and sat a Starbucks cup on my desk.

"One nonfat, no-whip mocha," she recited.

"Thanks!" I said. "What is that for?" Jocelyn is our HR assistant, but that doesn't mean she fetches coffee. She's the busiest person in our department, managing the thousands of tiny details that keep the office running.

"I figured you could use it today. Has Halloween insanity begun?"

"Insanity, check," I said. "One employee dressed as a feminine hygiene product." Jocelyn's eyes widened, and she leaned closer.

"Was she a pad?" she whispered. "With wings?" We both snickered, and I told her what happened.

Jocelyn lowered her voice, "Claire is super nice, but she loves to twist Shannon's tail. It wouldn't surprise me if she dressed that way just to get a reaction."

I shrugged. Yeah, it was possible. Who knew?

"Speaking of costumes, are you the Easter bunny?"

Jocelyn was wearing a slim white track suit with pink piping, a headband with fluffy white rabbit ears, and a necklace that looked like a carrot. Her pale brown hair was pulled back in a snug ponytail. She looked even younger than her twenty-five years.

"Oh no!" she said, frowning. "I'm the rabbit from the tortoise and the hare story. You know, how he was all fast and in shape?"

"Didn't the tortoise win?" I asked.

"Yeah," she smiled brightly as if she expected the question, "but it's not always about winning." Our front desk bell rang three times in rapid succession, and she raced off to answer it.

Dress code issues consumed most of the morning. Normally my generalist, Akiko, would have fielded these calls, but she was on a well-deserved vacation day.

By lunch, two employees in the billing office were wearing borrowed surgical scrubs to cover up 'inappropriate cleavage' and a Roman gladiator in internal medicine had been asked to put his toy sword in his car after a mock-battle had resulted in a bruised cheekbone. Three male nurses dressed as Teenage Mutant Ninja Turtles were sent to HR by their manager to get a photo taken for the company newsletter.

In between those interruptions, I reviewed resumes for our eight open nursing positions.

Recruiting can be satisfying. There's something primal about hunting down good candidates like you might stalk a deer through the forest. Although that might not be the best analogy, because instead of shooting candidates and gutting them on the hood of my car, I quiz them, flatter them, and offer them money. Still, I love the thrill of the hunt.

To sort the talented from the hopeful, I use a three-bucket system.

A = Exceeds Qualifications
B = Meets Qualifications
C = Smokin' Crack

A level candidates always get an interview. B level candidates get an interview if we don't have enough As in the pile. And the 'Smokin' Crack' category is reserved for the woefully unqualified, along with anyone who acts like an ass.

I was sorting resumes when Akiko's line rang.

"I want the status of my application," a gruff male voice barked.

My fingers tightened on the receiver, and I gave him the usual answer. "I'm sorry; we don't give application status over the phone. You can log into our website and see the status of every job you applied for."

"Look, lady, the website tells me nothing; it's a fat waste of my time. Connect me to the hiring manager."

"Let me find your record," I said.

I took his name and put him on hold. His resume wasn't bad, but we had other candidates who were more qualified.

I made a note in his profile: *Called to check on resume status. Was rude and impatient.* I knew my comment would make it even less likely he'd ever get an interview, and I didn't feel one iota of guilt. I figured if he was rude to me, he'd be rude to others too.

"Thanks for holding, Sir. I checked your profile, and it appears you haven't been selected for an interview. We have more qualified candidates. Anything else I can do for you?"

He hung up on me and I noted that in his applicant record too and placed his entire file in bucket C. Diagnosis: ass.

I ignored the rumbling in my stomach. I was hot on the heels of a qualified surgical nurse and I wanted to set up the interview right away. They're so rare they may as well be mythical.

Job Advertisement: Unicorn wanted for day shift in Gastroenterology. Bachelor of Science in Nursing preferred. Sparkly horn a plus.

I set up the interview and was feeling mighty fine when I saw an email come through from my boss.

> To: Katherine Voyzey
> From: Angela Griffin
> Subject: Come See Me ASAP.

Oh joy.

A thin tendril of dread threaded my gut and pulled itself taut. I glanced at the clock. Could I sneak out to lunch and deal with Angela later? No, I was being summoned, and it was best to get it over with.

I picked up a notepad and pencil and walked out of my office, past Jocelyn's desk, and through our lobby. A trio of job applicants looked up hopefully as I passed and sank back into their chairs after I passed.

"Angela's looking for you," Jocelyn said. She held the door open for me as I left the department. There was a cellophane bag of Halloween candy in one of her hands, and a take-away container from the cafeteria in the other.

"That's where I'm headed."

Jocelyn looked me over, shifted her food to the crook of her arm to free up a hand, and reached into her bag of treats. "Take one." She held out a brightly wrapped square. "Chocolate makes everything better."

I took one and smiled, reminded of how much I appreciate my little team. Jocelyn has a knack for making others feel better about themselves. It's one of the many reasons I hired her. Another reason?

She didn't call me repeatedly asking for the status of her application.

It takes ninety seconds to walk the long hallway that runs between human resources and our executive office suite. I used the interval to puzzle out what I'd screwed up this time. It couldn't be my costume. I knew Angela took a dim view of Halloween, so I toed the line by wearing a charcoal gray suit and a black dangly necklace adorned with spiders.

Angela joined Holy Heart one year ago, right after our previous Chief People Officer retired. On her first day, she handed me a list of twenty things I was doing wrong. I hadn't even met her yet, and she was telling me I was a screw-up.

Ever since then, she has gone out of her way to question my judgment. I look forward to our little talks like an ant looks forward to a boot.

Angela's assistant was on the phone when I arrived, but she must have been expecting me because she waved me in without comment. In her office, Angela was on her computer responding to email.

"I understand you had a visit from an employee this morning." She didn't turn to face me, so I was left to communicate with the back of her jacket.

Was she going to give me any additional hints as to what I had done wrong? No, even after she swiveled to face me, all I could sense was impatience.

"I had a few employees come in this morning. Can you tell me which one you are referring to?" I had my notepad out, and my pencil was poised to write. If I was writing something down, I didn't have to make eye contact.

Angela grimaced and crossed one dainty leg over the other. "Don't be coy, Katherine. An employee came in this morning wearing a very inappropriate costume, and you told her she could stay."

I winced. Did this woman have cameras implanted in my office? In my eye sockets? What the hell?

"Ah, you must mean Claire," I said, taking care to sound unruffled. "She did wear an inappropriate costume to work today. We discussed how she could modify it, and she asked Shannon if she could return to work."

Did Angela growl at me, or was it my imagination? No, it was just the sound of her clearing her throat. "You," she paused, pointing at me with her index finger, "should not be in the business of helping employees break the rules. You need to set an example."

"I wasn't encouraging her to break the rules. I told Claire she needed to ask—"

"Bad judgment," she interrupted. "You're not her friend. You're a member of the management team. The next time this happens, God forbid, tell the person to stop questioning their manager and to go home and change. If they don't like it, I hear Virginia Mason is hiring."

I looked up from the page and tried to meet her steely gaze with something approximating obedience. "I understand, Angela." And I did. I understood that she was being impossible, and it was my job to be quiet and suck it up. "Is there anything else you need from me?"

"No." She swiveled back to face her desk and pick up her phone. I was dismissed.

CHAPTER THREE

WHENEVER I TANGLE WITH ANGELA, I feel it in my gut for hours. By six thirty in the evening, the knot in my stomach was gone, but I was still replaying my conversation with Claire, trying to figure out what I'd done wrong.

I knew the answer, but I didn't like it. According to my boss, whenever an employee makes a mistake we should rub their nose in it. Once they've been properly humiliated, we can move on.

The problem? I'm not particularly interested in humiliating people, sending them a message, or being the official corporate bitch. Angela wants me to be that person, and I keep resisting. Hence her regular reminders that I'm a disappointment.

I reached into the candy bowl I'd spirited off Jocelyn's desk. My fingers brushed bare glass, and my stomach growled. It was full dark outside my window, and I needed to eat something that didn't come packaged in a foil wrapper. Besides, Milo would want dinner, too.

I was fishing my keys out of my purse when the phone rang.

"Holy Heart, this is Kat. How can I help you?"

"Is this the HR director?"

Her voice was clear, formal, and unfamiliar. So much for dinner, I thought. This call had all the markers of an after-hours sexual harassment complaint.

"Yes. Who am I speaking with?"

"Oh! Thank God you're still here!" Now I could hear the relief in her voice, and the words tumbled out in a rush. "This is Mary Cisneros from the ER. We have a situation down here in medical records."

My brain whirled the pieces around, but they didn't add up to a coherent picture. Why was an emergency room nurse in medical records? And what did this have to do with HR?

"What happened?"

"One of the clerks has been shot. She's dead, and I've got staff down here. We don't know what to do with them."

Then a moment later, "Kat, are you still there?"

My mind was a blank, but the part of me that was shocked stepped to one side so the rest of me could deal.

"Where are you? And who else is there?"

"I'm in the hallway outside the records room. Two EMTs are inside with the—the woman who died. Her coworkers found her, and they're here with me."

"Okay. Here's what I want you to do. Take the clerks to the ER. Find a safe place for them to wait. I'll call the police, and then I'll meet you outside the records room. Go now. I'll be right there."

Shaking fingers pressed 9-1-1 on my cell phone. A voice answered, and I spoke, sounding much calmer than I felt. My feet moved me toward the exit.

The police were on their way. So was I.

I WALKED AS FAST AS I could without drawing attention to myself. God knows what was written on my face, and the sight of the HR director sprinting down the halls might bring unwanted attention. I pressed my security pass against the black pad at the stairwell until it beeped. I trotted down the stairs. The echoes of my footsteps raced out in front of me.

On the lower level, the hallway lights had been dimmed for the evening, but the door to the records room was wide open and a bright square of light splashed onto the hallway tiles outside. There was no sign of the nurse, so I walked up to the doorway, took a breath, and stepped inside.

At first, I saw nothing out of the ordinary. The medical records department was laid out like a library, only with file folders instead of books. Floor-to-ceiling racks formed long rows, and our file clerks move up and down the aisles with carts, pulling patient charts or putting them back in their proper places.

I stepped behind the front counter and walked around the first row. Down at the end of the aisle, I saw her.

Two men in dark blue EMT jackets were standing near a body on the ground; one of them was muttering into a handheld radio. The victim—a woman—was lying face up on the blue carpet.

A plastic respirator mask and a tangle of plastic tubing obscured her face, but I could tell she was petite, and her short brown hair was touched with silver. She wore a sweatshirt with a picture of a jack-o'-lantern on it. As I moved closer, I felt a prickle of recognition.

There was a dark stain seeping into the blue carpet next to the body. Nearby, a chrome file cart was on its side. A few dozen patient charts were scattered on the floor like forgotten playing cards. I felt the ground wobble beneath my feet.

One of the EMTs spotted me. "Miss, you can't be in here." He moved to stand between me and the body, blocking it from view.

"I'm from HR. Mary just called me."

"It's okay, Mark." I recognized that voice from the telephone and turned around.

"Kat? I'm Mary." Her hazel eyes narrowed, and she stepped forward to place a hand on my arm. "And you need to sit down."

She deftly maneuvered me into a nearby chair. The ground stopped moving.

"Thanks," I said. Mary took the chair opposite me and leaned forward to speak quietly.

"Take deep breaths. That isn't an easy thing to see, and you were going into shock."

I obediently took air into my lungs, held it, and then blew it out. I'd never seen a dead body before. Not even my father's body, after he'd died in his sleep. The doctor had offered, but I'd said no. There are things you can't unsee, and I didn't want that image floating around in my memory.

"Good, your color's returning," Mary said. She patted my knee. "Did you call the police?"

"Yes, I called 9-1-1. They said they'd be here in a few minutes."

"Good. I think the EMTs called them too. I forgot they can do that."

"What happened?"

"I didn't see. But what I gather is that the other two file clerks were elsewhere, and when they came back, they found her. One of them came running into the ER to get help. We sent the two EMTs right over, but she was already gone."

"Is it Anna Vasquez?" I hoped that I was wrong but I knew I wasn't.

"I'm afraid so. Do you know her?"

My heart sank. "Yeah."

"I'm so sorry," Mary reached out and squeezed my hand in her own. It was warm and surprisingly strong.

I squeezed back and then pulled away. Our hospital was too big to know every employee by name, but Anna stood out. The good ones always do. And the jerks, I suppose. It was the people in the middle that tended to fade from the mind. The invisibles. Anna Vasquez one of the good ones, a real team player.

"Every year we ask for volunteers for the employee picnic," I said. "It's one of those pain-in-the-butt assignments no one wants, but Anna always managed the children's activities. She ends up babysitting the whole time, but she seemed to love it."

In fact, the last time I'd seen Anna was at the company picnic in late August. She was applying a Band-Aid to the knee of a young boy. He'd been crying, but whatever she was whispering in his ear was making him giggle.

I thought I might cry, but my tear ducts were out of sync with the rest of me. That was fine. There were too many people around, anyway, and too much to do.

A door slammed out in the hallway. Mary went to the doorway and looked outside, but there must have been nothing to see; she returned quickly.

"The women who found her are fine," she said. "I don't think they saw much, but they're understandably upset. I put them in an exam room and Dr. Conway is keeping an eye on them until you get there. The EMTs will wait here until the police arrive unless they get another call."

Mary was still standing, waiting for something. I realized that she expected me to follow her to the ER.

"I don't know what to say to them."

She nodded, but didn't offer any advice. "Come on. You're fine, and I've got patients waiting."

Mary walked me through a series of doors, past the emergency room reception desk, and toward the exam rooms in the back.

It must have been a busy night because the ER was full. In one room a couple was arguing loudly about the cost of an X-ray. In another, a child was wailing. Finally, we arrived at a nondescript door; Mary knocked softly before opening it.

There were three people inside. The physician's stool was occupied by Dr. Conway, the head of emergency medicine. A vigorous man in his early sixties, he must have been expecting us because he stood as soon as I walked in.

In the plastic chairs along one wall, two women sat with white hospital blankets draped over their shoulders. Bridget Chan I recognized right away with her steel gray hair and double wrist braces. Her eyes flicked toward me, but she remained expressionless.

Next to her sat a younger woman with dark hair and a swollen nose. The plastic name badge peeking out from the blanket indicated she was an employee, but the name was hidden.

As soon as I was inside, Dr. Conway gave me his seat. I thought he was being polite until he moved toward the doorway with a relieved expression.

"Bridget, Sally, this is Kat from human resources. She's going to stay with you while the police talk to you, and then make sure you get a ride home tonight, okay?"

"Thank you, Doctor," Bridget murmured.

The door shut with a loud click, and I put my hands in my lap. I looked at the women, and they looked at me. Bridget's reserve broke open like a dam, and tears streamed down her face. She didn't wipe them away.

"Someone murdered Anna."

"I know," I said, feeling my eyes sting in response to her tears.

The three of us waited for a long time without talking. I probably should have said something, something comforting, but everything I came up with sounded pointless. Finally, a sharp knock on the door heralded the arrival of the Seattle PD.

CHAPTER FOUR

"HELLO. I'M DETECTIVE SUSAN PATTERSON and this is my partner, Detective Evans."

The woman who spoke so confidently looked nothing like the cops you see on TV. Stocky and not very tall, she was probably in her early fifties. Her thick brown hair was plaited in tiny braids and swept into a high bun. She wore a navy-blue pantsuit and a necklace of colorful plastic pony beads that looked like they'd been strung by a child. She looked more like someone's grandmother than an officer of the law.

Her partner nodded at us from the doorway but remained silent. At least two decades younger than his counterpart, he was apparently there to observe.

Detective Patterson took the remaining seat in the room and asked us for our full names, addresses, and phone numbers. Once she'd documented those, she put her notebook away in her jacket pocket.

"Please tell me what you saw," she said.

Bridget responded first. "Sally and I were working the swing shift from two to eleven," she explained. "At six, I went to the cafeteria to get dinner before they closed. When I got back, I heard Sally yelling for help."

The younger woman nodded and wiped her nose on the sleeve of her cardigan. "I left a few minutes after Bridget did. Anna told me Dr. Carter needed some charts, like right away, so I took them over to pediatrics."

I expected the detective to ask a follow-up question, but instead she waited.

"I wasn't gone long," Sally added. "Maybe twenty minutes? I didn't see anything wrong at first. I thought Anna was filing in the back." Sally's eyes filled with tears and her voice caught. "But she was on the ground and she wasn't moving. The file cart was on top of her, and I thought she fell. Maybe had a stroke?

"I moved the cart; she was bleeding. I called her name, but she didn't answer. Her eyes were open, but she was gone." Sally covered her face with both hands, and Bridget put her arm around her.

I reached into the cabinet above my chair to pull down a box of tissues.

Bridget spoke next. "I got back, and Sally was screaming; when I got inside she was kneeling next to Anna on the ground. Anna wasn't breathing, and I told Sally to run to the ER and get help. I attempted CPR, but I don't know how helpful it was. There was so much blood."

She shuddered and looked at her hands, which were clean.

"Help arrived within a minute or two—those guys were really fast—and Mary brought us in here..." Bridget looked over at the detective. "I overheard the EMTs say Anna was shot twice in the chest. Is that true?"

"Our team is in there right now," Patterson answered. "They'll come in and give us an update soon. Did either of you see anyone else in the area tonight?"

"No, it was quiet," Sally said. Bridget nodded.

"Do you have any idea who might want to hurt Anna?"

They shook their heads.

"Did you hear a gunshot or a loud bang? It could have sounded like a slammed door or something dropped on the ground."

Neither of them remembered hearing anything out of the ordinary.

Sally hung her head in her hands. Bridget rubbed her eyes. They looked like they needed a break from the questioning.

"Detective," I asked, "have you searched the area? Are we safe here?"

"I've got a team on that. Let's check in with them." She looked over at her partner, who nodded and disappeared into the hallway.

Sally's voice was so low that I needed to lean in to hear her. "I shouldn't have left her alone."

"Oh honey, listen to me," Patterson said, reaching out to pat her on the knee. "It's lucky you were away. If you'd been there, you might've been hurt too. I don't think your friend would've wanted that."

"She said I should hurry. That we didn't want to keep Dr. Carter waiting." Sally blotted her eyes with a wad of tissues.

"It sounds like she was very conscientious about her work," I said.

Bridget smiled. "Anna cares about everyone. She's two years younger than me, but she treated all of us like her kids. She was always making sure we were eating healthy, taking our breaks…"

"Does Anna have family nearby?" Detective Patterson pulled out her notebook again.

Sally nodded, but Bridget spoke first, "She has custody of her two grandchildren, elementary school age I think. Crap. What's going to happen to them?"

"Do you know where they are tonight?" The detective asked.

"At her brother's house," Bridget said. "Her brother and his wife watch them while she works. What's his name, Sal?"

"Thomas," Sally said. "I think he's watching the kids at Anna's house tonight."

"We'll make sure the kids are safe, I promise," Detective Patterson said.

A uniformed officer arrived at the doorway and waited to be acknowledged. Detective Evans was back too. He moved to one side to let him in. The exam room was getting crowded.

"What have you found?" Patterson asked.

"We've completed the sweep of this building. No weapon on the scene. No sign of the assailant. No note. There's a pharmacy storeroom next to the crime scene. It looks like someone tried to bust it open with a crowbar, but they were interrupted. No security cameras that we can see. We'll be wrapped up here in thirty minutes."

He scribbled a note on a pad of paper and handed it to the detective, whose eyes flicked over it. She stuck it in her jacket pocket.

Detective Patterson stood up. "Whoever did this is long gone. Sally, Bridget, I'll have Detective Evans drive you home. I may have more questions for you, in which case I'll be in touch. Thank you for your help tonight, and I am so sorry for your loss."

As she reached over to shake their hands, she did look truly sorry. They thanked her and allowed the uniformed officer to lead them out.

Detective Patterson turned to me. "You're from corporate, right? Can you add anything to their statements?"

I filled her in on what I'd seen, which wasn't much. She nodded. "We need to notify next of kin. Can you get me that information?"

"Sure. Follow me." As I led her out of the emergency room, I wondered what was on the handwritten note.

OUR HOSPITAL HAS TWO FACES.

In daylight, it's all hustle. Patients are walking around or being wheeled from place to place. Visitors arrive, embrace one another, and chatter like jaybirds. There's the sharp whine of coffee beans being pulverized at the Starbucks, the ka-ching of the cash register where volunteers sold flowers in the gift shop, and the occasional crackle of pages on the intercom.

At night, the hospital has a different feel. Detective Patterson and I walked down the long, dim hallway without speaking. The only sounds were our footsteps, and the storefronts and shops were dark, their metal gates pulled down. A single electric candle burned at the entrance to the chapel, reminding the faithful that God is always ready to listen.

A nice concept, for sure, but it provided me no comfort. At work I kept my non-believer status to myself, figuring it was easier that way. The values of our hospital were good ones: Humility, service, and compassion—I could get behind that. But the notion that Anna now dwelled in some transcendent paradise? I couldn't buy it.

Sometimes I envied the faithful. It must be nice to believe everything will be all right.

Thankfully, the detective didn't feel the need to fill up the silence with small talk. In the wake of what happened, the quiet felt appropriate.

I unlocked the heavy wooden door to my department and flipped on a few lights.

"Come on in. I'll get her file for you."

She looked around the room and paused beneath the large maple and brass crucifix hanging on the wall.

"I thought it was illegal to mix religion and human resources."

"We're a Catholic hospital," I explained. "Faith is an important part of our culture."

"Do you only hire Catholics? That must be hard. Seattleites aren't particularly devout."

I shook my head. "We don't discriminate on the basis of religion, but we have all new hires sign a document saying they'll abide by our organizational values. There are plenty of Catholics in Seattle, but we won't turn down a great surgeon or nurse simply because they worship differently. Or not at all."

"Ah," she said, and left it at that.

I retrieved a ring of keys from the lock box in the hall and walked back to the room that houses our personnel files, copier, and mailboxes. I unlocked the file drawer labeled V-Z and pulled out Anna's personnel file and laid it flat on the counter. Then I pried open the long brass brads holding the pages in place and lifted the stack of paper free.

On her emergency contact sheet, I found the phone number and address for her brother, Thomas Vasquez. I ran a copy of that page, along with the front page of her file, containing her current domicile.

"You don't need the rest of this stuff, do you? Performance reviews and so on?"

"No, emergency contact and address are fine." She crossed her arms, leaned against the wall, and looked at me as if making her mind up about something.

"Do you drug test here?" she asked.

"Yes, upon hire; after hire we test only upon suspicion of use." I looked up at her. "Why?"

"Just curious," she said, changing the subject. "Say, I'm likely to have more questions for you all tomorrow or the next day. If I contact you, can you get Evans and me a private room so we can talk to your employees?"

"Sure. What was on the paper you stuck in your pocket?"

"Why?"

"Just curious," I said, in the same casual tone she'd used.

I saw a flash of amusement in her eyes, but she responded with a question of her own. "How well did you know the victim?"

"Not well. We spoke a few times per year, and I liked her."

"Any work issues or personality conflicts?"

"Not that I'm aware of. She had a good reputation, and I don't remember any problems associated with her. Say, don't you take people down to the precinct to talk to them? Or is that just how they do it on TV?"

She snorted a laugh and shook her head. "You mean the good-cop, bad-cop stuff? Nah." She thrust her thumbs through her belt loops. "Most perps are too smart for those cheesy moves, and they're unnecessary, anyway. We have interview rooms at the precinct, but they're usually booked. Too many damn staff meetings."

I placed the pages she wanted on our copy machine and hit the print button. A hum signaled the machine was warming up. "I know what you mean. Half the time when we're in a meeting there's someone tapping a foot outside the door, waiting for us to vacate."

"Besides," she said, "I doubt any of your people are involved. Why stress them out by bringing them to the precinct? No, I'll call you, and we can wrap up our questions all at once."

"My boss will probably want me to sit in. Is that all right?" That was an understatement. Angela would want to wrap the entire building with a human fence made out of attorneys. I wasn't looking forward to that phone call.

"Yeah, that should be fine," Patterson said. She took the photocopies from me with a small sigh, and it occurred to me her night was only starting. Next, she had to give the Vasquez family the worst news they'd ever hear. The detective squared her shoulders, and my opinion of her rose another notch.

I walked her out and locked up the department, then called Angela.

CHAPTER FIVE

THE NEXT MORNING, MY ALARM blared at five a.m. I hit the snooze button twice before dragging myself out from under the comforter.

The scalding water in the shower turned my pale skin pink, and I wished it could wash away more than dirt and sweat. All night I'd tossed and turned, dreaming about the murder, except that in my dreams the body belonged to my sister, Dori.

On the kitchen counter I saw Detective Patterson's business card, where I'd left it the previous night. I needed to get to the office, fast. Today we'd need to tell the staff what happened, and that meant we needed a plan.

Milo followed me out of the bedroom and did his hungry dance, which consists of purring like a cement mixer and hurling himself forcibly against my shins. I grabbed a clean cat dish out of the dishwasher, poured him a small mountain of kibble, and then grabbed the remote control to flip on the morning news.

There was one report on Boeing contract negotiations, five minutes of traffic reporting (consensus: traffic = bad), and a cheerful confirmation that the rain we'd been subjected to would continue for another decade or so. Nothing about the hospital, at least not yet.

Milo was sitting on my wool coat, one leg high in the air, licking his rear end.

I shooed him off. Bad enough that I was a single woman with a cat; the last thing I needed was an outfit covered in fur to cement my status as a thirty-something spinster. Milo shot me a look of disgust and sauntered into the bedroom in search of other clean laundry to sit on.

"I'll be home early tonight," I told him. "And I'll bring us takeout."

I heard his meow echo down the hall and felt a pang of guilt. With my long hours at work I'd been an inattentive cat owner lately. I would have gotten Milo a feline friend, but he seemed to prefer being king of the castle.

My voicemail light was blinking. I hit play and sat down to pull on my boots.

"Kat, this is your Mom." Agatha Voyzey's strident voice was unmistakable. "You haven't called me in three weeks, but I know you're busy."

She sounded matter of fact about the latter part, but I felt bad anyway.

"Dori's having a cookout on Saturday. Lord knows why anyone would barbecue in the pouring rain, but there it is. We'll see you at three. Bring a dish. And a date. Call me back."

I stood up and checked myself in the mirror. Dark circles under the eyes, chestnut brown hair that was more frizzy than curly, and a distinct look of annoyance on my face. Where was I going to find a date? In between the stacks of paper on my desk? Perhaps I'd have a hot and heavy affair with our annual EEO-1 report.

From my condo just off Broadway, I drove downhill toward downtown. As soon as I cleared the oak trees and brick buildings, the city burst into view.

It was dark and cold that morning, but the skyline was beautiful. The evening fog was gone, and the Space Needle gleamed white like a beacon, nestled amongst the glittering towers of the city. Recent rains gave the streets a soft glow that even the overcast sky couldn't diminish.

At the hospital, the employee parking lot was nearly empty. As soon as I walked past the executive suite, Angela's hawkish voice grabbed me from behind.

"Katherine, is that you? Come see me."

Angela's office was as dark as the ICU late at night. The only light was coming from her computer screen, but it gave off just enough brightness to show she had a set of dark circles under her eyes to match mine. Had she slept?

"We're lucky," she said without taking her eyes from the screen. "The media either hasn't heard about our little tragedy, or they don't care. Let's hope it stays that way."

Lucky? Little tragedy? Did she have no idea how she sounded?

Angela half-rose from her chair to reach for something on top of her printer. She handed me a sheet of paper, still warm from the fuser.

It read as follows:

To: All Staff
From: Gary Westerman, CEO

We lost a valued employee and friend last night. Anna Vasquez was injured during a botched robbery at the hospital and later succumbed to her injuries. She and her family are in our prayers.

Your safety and security are our top priority. While the police believe this was an isolated incident, we are taking every precaution. Security has been posted throughout the hospital, and we're cooperating fully with the Seattle Police Department as they investigate this tragic incident.

Yours in Christ,
Gary

"Did you write this?" I asked.

Angela nodded.

"The police confirmed it was a robbery?" I was surprised at the certainty in the email.

Angela shrugged. "That woman detective implied it. I spoke to her last night. This city is overrun with drug addicts and petty criminals, so it's no surprise our pharmacy was a target."

Scrutinizing the page again, I picked up a pen and pointed it at the page. "May I?"

"Go ahead," she said.

After taking a moment to compose my thoughts, I added the following.

> *As we take care of our patients during this difficult day, we must also care for ourselves. HR will be sending each manager information about our Employee Assistance Program (EAP) hotline, and spiritual counseling is available to anyone who requests it.*

I handed the paper back to her, and she read it. "The personal touch is good. You'll send that information out now?" she asked.

"Yes, I'll send it as soon as I see Gary's message go out."

She nodded. "Good. Go watch for it."

I went to my office; when the email came through I wasn't surprised to see Angela's last-minute addition.

> *Out of respect for the Vasquez family, you are instructed not to speak to the media about this tragedy.*

She should know better, I thought. Telling people not to talk would only make tongues wag faster.

At seven fifteen, Jocelyn arrived at work. She balanced three fat orientation binders on one arm and carried a large box of doughnuts in the other.

She must have seen something in my expression because she dropped everything on her desk and asked what happened. I told her. When I was done, Jocelyn crossed herself. "God rest her soul, that poor woman. How can I help?"

"Assemble the team in the conference room as soon as Akiko gets in. We'll have our hands full today, and we need a plan."

CHAPTER SIX

THE HR TEAM IS SMALL, five people including myself, and to look at us you'd think we had nothing in common. Given our differences in background and personality, it was surprising we worked together as well as we did.

Davis, our benefits manager, was seated at the foot of the conference table with his hands folded. Our most conservative coworker, both in appearance and attitude, he dressed like a banker and avoided all vices, including chocolate, alcohol, and swearing. I liked Davis—he had a kind heart—but I imagined he prayed for my salvation daily.

Akiko, our generalist and my right hand, stood out because of her goth-professional clothing, thick black eyeliner, and rapid-fire way of talking. Smart and hard-working, she handles the day-to-day problems that come through our department.

Erin was our trainer, and she was both capable and a pain in my ass. Her mouth had gotten me in trouble with Angela more times than I could count. But she had a knack for saying what everyone else was thinking, but too afraid to bring up, which made her invaluable.

We each had our specialty, but Jocelyn was the glue that held us all together: fielding calls, smoothing ruffled feelings, and picking up balls whenever they got dropped. I'd be lost without her.

As I pulled the conference room door shut behind me, the team looked at me expectantly.

"Did everyone read Gary's email?" I asked.

"Yes," Akiko said. "It's terrible. How could a murder happen here?"

"Murders can happen anywhere," Erin said. "I heard she was shot four times in the chest, and you saw the body. Did you? That must have been awful."

"Who told you?" It occurred to me that the EMTs knew about what happened, and the ER nurses, and probably the security staff. The rumor mill worked fast at Holy Heart.

"I got it from a housekeeper. She said everyone's talking about it." Erin shrugged.

"Did any of you know Anna?" We needed a plan, but that could wait if one of us was grieving a friend.

"Not well," Davis said slowly, "but I met her. She came in a few weeks ago to ask for benefits information, and we talked for a while. She was a nice lady."

Jocelyn nodded. "I recognize her name of course, but we haven't met, at least not that I remember." She frowned. "Shelby will be devastated."

"Shit!" I said, banging my hand on the table.

Davis winced, and everyone else stared.

"Sorry." I shot Davis an apologetic glance. "I didn't even think about Shelby when this all went down. I should've called her." Between talking to the police and keeping Angela updated, I hadn't even considered Anna's manager. My stomach twisted, and I rose to my feet to grab the phone. If one of my people had been killed, I'd be inconsolable. How could I have been so careless?

Akiko stalled me. "I agree you should check in. Absolutely. But she gets in at six, so she's already seen the email and been here for a few hours working. You may as well finish up with us. Then I'll cover your phone, and you can head down in person."

She was right; I could make amends later.

"I'll give you the facts, and then we can talk about what needs to be done." I described the events of the previous evening, starting with the phone call.

"So, it was a robbery? How did they get in without a keycard?" Erin asked.

"I don't know, but it looks like someone tried to break into the pharmacy. It's a mystery as to why they were in medical records. Perhaps Anna tried to stop them? Unfortunately, we don't have any security cameras."

"Did the clerks see anything suspicious?" Akiko asked.

"They were out of the department when it happened, and it was too late to help when they got back. She'd already passed away."

Jocelyn started to cry. Davis touched his crucifix and muttered something. Akiko handed Joss a tissue and put an arm around her shoulders.

"Jesus, Mary, and Joseph," Jocelyn wiped her nose. "Her poor family!"

Davis asked if her family had been notified, and I told him Detective Patterson had gone to see them late last night.

"Our employees won't feel safe," Erin said, highlighting one of my worries. "What if they refuse to come to work? Until we know who did this, there's no guarantee it won't happen again. People are going to ask: Am I next?"

"We've added security, right?" Davis asked, twisting the wedding ring on his finger. "That's what the email said."

I nodded. "There's no reason to believe this was anything but an isolated incident, but Greg and the executive team agree better safe than sorry."

"Did you talk to the police?" Erin asked pointedly. "What's the proof this was an isolated incident? Are you sure this isn't wishful thinking on the part of management?"

Erin had a point.

"I talked to the detective in charge. She said they'll be back with questions, and we need to make our conference room available. And I'll sit in on those conversations, so our employees aren't alone."

"Did anyone see the shooter?" Erin pursued.

"It doesn't sound like it."

"Will we hear anything from the police, once they've found the monster who did it?" Akiko asked. Her expression was as dark as her outfit.

"I assume they'll be in touch with Anna's family, but I'm not sure if they'll tell us anything. I have the detective's business card; she asked us to contact her if we hear anything useful."

We sat in silence for a few moments. No doubt everyone was processing this information in their own way. Jocelyn's head popped up from the table at the sound of the ringing phone, her eyes puffy.

"Let it go to voicemail," I said. "We're almost done here."

"How can we help?" Akiko asked, ever to the point. "Answer the phones, keep people calm?"

I nodded. "Here's what I suggest. Davis, I'll go see Shelby, and I'd like to give her hard copies of our EAP information for the file clerks. Can you run those for me?"

"Yes. I'll do it now. And I'll call our vendor; maybe they can send grief counselors on-site." He pushed back his chair and stood up.

"Jocelyn, we may get a lot of calls from managers with questions about the murder. Employees are going to be afraid, and managers may need help in responding. I'd ask all of you to avoid going into the grisly details, but be as encouraging as you can. If they need resources, please connect them. Anything else, forward to me or Akiko."

"Okay."

"Akiko, use your best judgment with the managers. I imagine they'll need advice on comforting people, and information on the investigation. You can share that it seems to be a robbery gone bad, that we've added security, and that we'll do what we can to support Anna's family."

"Makes sense," she said.

"One last thing, everyone. Make sure you know who you're speaking to if someone calls. If we get any questions from the media, those go straight to Angela. Don't speak to any outsiders on behalf of the company. She wants to handle those calls personally. Now what am I forgetting?" I asked.

"Father Callahan," Jocelyn said. "He'll want to provide spiritual counseling. Maybe even schedule a service for Anna."

"Joss, would you call him? See if he knows if Anna was Catholic, and if a service would be appropriate."

"Sure, he'll be glad to help."

"Thanks, everyone. I'm going to medical records to talk to Shelby, but I'll be back soon."

The meeting was over, but we lingered in the conference room. Jocelyn cried again, and Davis comforted her. Akiko was calm and focused, making sure everyone had what they needed to make it through the day. Even Erin, my talented troublemaker, didn't make a single snide comment.

I cast a glance back at them as I left, feeling relieved they were all safe. And guilty, because not everyone at Holy Heart was so lucky.

CHAPTER SEVEN

I DIDN'T WANT TO GO back to the scene of the crime. Guilt was making my heart so heavy that I could almost feel it dragging behind me as I walked.

Had Shelby arrived at work and found out one of her employees had been murdered by reading an email? By seeing the stain on the carpet? Even brushing up against that thought made my heart ache.

On the way to medical records I paused at the statue of our hospital's founder, Sister Constance. I've always liked that spot, which sits in a quiet corner of the hospital, near a fountain.

Sister Constance is smiling and everyone at Holy Heart Medical Center knows the reason why. After Seattle burned to the ground in June of 1889, the wise men of the city decided to rebuild on stronger ground by bringing in millions of tons of dirt and burying the old buildings. The new city was built literally on top of the old one.

The order of the Holy Heart knew the city needed a hospital, but they had no money or influence to obtain the land they'd need to build one. And after trying to track down the city's mayor unsuccessfully for months, Constance found him in a private poker game one afternoon, where she launched into her request for land to build a hospital.

The mayor, well into his fourth whiskey, announced with a laugh that he would donate the land if she could beat him in a game of poker.

Three hours later, Sister Constance walked out with the deed to the land, the mayor's gold pocket watch, and enough cash to buy the supplies for the foundation of the first building. The rest, as they say, is history.

I looked up at the statue and whispered, "I don't know what I'm doing." Sister Constance smiled at me—her expression so lifelike—and it occurred to me she might not have known what she was doing either. The heaviness in my heart lifted, just a little.

I took the elevator down to the basement level, feeling apprehensive about what I would find. Downstairs, a jumble of voices spilled out into the hallway. Moving toward the sound, I paused at the pharmacy door. Thick white scrapes wreathed the doorknob where our intruder had tried to break in. I tried turning the knob, but the door was locked.

Next to the pharmacy, the medical records department was also shut and locked. A sign directed staff to call a phone number if they needed access to the files in that room.

The noise picked back up, and I located the source: a break room just down the hall. A tall woman with her hair in a long red braid waved me inside.

"Everyone, it's Kat. Come on in, dear. Sally, can you find her a chair?"

"Thank you," I said, trying to remember her name. She must have noticed my look of concentration because she introduced herself.

"Amy," she reminded me. "Medical records clerk two. We met at the picnic. There's a chair for you."

It seemed the entire medical records team was crammed in there. Bridget was sitting near the far wall beside the microwave, passing around a plate of chocolate chip cookies. Of the women in the room (and they were all women), two-thirds were past middle age, and four were wearing black wrist braces. Carpal tunnel is a constant threat when your job consists of filing and sorting pages for an eight-hour shift.

Bridget walked over and patted me on the back with one hand. "Kat, you came! I'm so glad."

I looked around for Shelby, but didn't see her. "Is Shelby here?"

"Yeah, she'll be back in a minute. She went to check messages," Sally said from her seat near the fridge. She took a sip from her mug of coffee and sat it down on the table with a loud click. The side of the mug read "5 Years of Service" in gold script against a dark blue background.

"Ladies, don't take this the wrong way," I said, "but why are you at work today? If you needed time to recoup from what happened last night, no one would blame you."

Bridget ran her fingers through her short hair, "It's better to be here. I couldn't stop thinking about what happened. We called a meeting."

One clerk (Martha by her name tag) spoke up, "We all loved Anna; she was like a big sister to us. How could this happen at Holy Heart? It seems impossible."

The door clicked shut behind me and I turned to see that Shelby Cooper had arrived. She deftly squeezed herself behind the occupied chairs and took the last remaining seat.

"Thanks for coming, Kat," Shelby said. She sounded tired, in contrast to her team, which was full of something—frustration?

"I called HR, but they said you were already on your way." She flipped her long blond hair over her shoulder and rubbed the back of her neck with one hand.

"I wanted to check in on everyone and see how you are doing." I frowned. "And to say how sorry I am for not calling you last night. I feel terrible; and I should have been more thoughtful."

"No harm done. Bridget called me last night and told me you were talking to the police. You had a lot to deal with; I wouldn't expect you to think of everything."

She looked at her team; apparently this was their meeting to run. The clerks looked at Bridget.

"We called this meeting because we want to help." Bridget said, looking at her boss. "We want to do something for Anna's family."

Shelby chewed on the end of her pen. "To be honest, I'm not sure what more we can do at this point. We're sending flowers from all of us."

Several members of the team nodded at this.

"And I don't know about the funeral service, but I'll find out," Shelby continued. "Does anyone know who will take care of her grandkids?"

"Her brother, probably," Bridget said. "Her daughter is out of the picture." Several clerks nodded at this, and a couple of them leaned toward one another to whisper.

"Are they sure it was a robbery, Katherine?" Shelby asked. "What did the police say?"

"Not much. They searched the area last night and found nothing. No weapon, no criminals, but signs of a break-in at the pharmacy."

"That's not all the police are saying," Sally flung the words out like she was tossing down a gauntlet.

Everyone stared at her.

"What do you mean?" I asked.

"I talked to Thomas this morning—Anna's brother. The police believe she was selling drugs, and that's why she was shot."

Sounds of dismay and anger rose up around the table.

"That's ridiculous," Martha snapped.

"Are they mental?" Amy demanded. "Thomas must have told them about Beth."

I didn't know who that was, but I remembered the detective's question about drug screening. Perhaps they'd suspected more than they'd let on.

Sally rolled her eyes. "That's how it goes. The police see she's Latina, and they assume it's her fault."

"But Detective Patterson is black," Bridget said. "Cops have a reputation for profiling, but I doubt she's a racist."

"Black people can be racist, too, you know," Amy responded. "My cousin married a black guy, and he said that—"

I jumped in to shift the conversation to more productive ground. "Hold on. Catch me up, please. Who is Beth, and why do the police think Anna was selling drugs?"

Bridget spoke, and everyone leaned in to listen. "Beth is Anna's daughter. She fell in with a bad crowd after high school and got addicted to cocaine, and later, to meth. She dropped the kids off for a visit one day and never came back."

Sally nodded. "That's why Anna hates drugs. She blamed them for ruining her daughter's life, and for destroying her family. There's no way she would mess with that stuff. Not in a million years!"

"Then why do the police think Anna was involved?" I asked.

"They asked her brother if she had prescriptions for Oxytocin, Valium, and a half-dozen other things," Sally said. "Then they said Anna had a bunch of pills in her purse, and even more in her car, along with cocaine and some cash."

The clerks fell silent.

"No," Amy whispered.

"I don't believe it," Shelby said.

"Well, the police do," Sally said. "According to Thomas, the police hinted Anna was involved in the pharmacy break-in and they suggested one of her 'accomplices' shot her."

Bridget scowled. "Great. The family gets devastated twice. First Thomas finds out his sister is murdered; then the police try to say she's a criminal. That's not right."

I looked around the table and saw anger, sadness, and shock.

Shelby looked like she was thinking hard. And if she was surprised, she was hiding it well. Perhaps she knew something the rest of the team didn't?

"Listen," I said, "if you tell me Anna hated drugs and she wouldn't touch them, I believe you." The group relaxed a little in response my words. "And I spent some time with the detective last night; she seems like a fair and compassionate person. Although I agree the police's theory sounds out of character for Anna."

But how often do we truly know someone, I wondered? My job gave me some insight into human nature, but it hadn't stopped me from being duped in my personal life in the past. When we care about someone, we tend to see what we wish to see. It can blind us to what's right in front of us.

Bridget nodded. "What can we do to help the family?"

"Yes, we want to help." This from an elderly woman pouring coffee in the back of the room.

"We owe it to Anna," Amy said.

"She deserves justice." Martha agreed.

I caught Shelby's eye, but she just raised her shoulders in a tiny shrug. She didn't know what to say, either. I fell back on the facts. "We've added security down here for all shifts. It seems unlikely anything will happen again, but we are not taking any chances."

There were nods around the table.

"As for the investigation, I suggest we let the police do their jobs, but let's also keep our eyes out. If you hear or see anything that might shed light on this situation, call me. The detective said she'd be back to ask follow-up questions, so if you're needed, we'll call you."

The team wanted so badly to help, but I had no good ideas for them. We closed the meeting with some announcements. Shelby reiterated that she'd follow-up about funeral arrangements. I took a few moments to hand out materials on our Employee Assistance Program.

The meeting broke up, and the clerks drifted toward the door. Some returned to the file room while those who weren't on duty walked toward the elevators.

I was on my way to Shelby's office when Sally surprised me by reaching out to give me a hug.

"Thanks for coming, Katherine. It means a lot to us."

"I only wish there was something I could do to help." I wanted to. But how?

"You can help us clear Anna's name," Sally said, answering my thoughts. "She doesn't deserve any of this. Not being murdered. Not having her name drug through the mud. She was..." Sally's face crumpled, and she paused long enough to compose herself. "She was one of us."

We looked at each other until the ding of the elevator nearby broke the spell.

CHAPTER EIGHT

I TRIED NOT TO LOOK at the spot on the floor where Anna had died, but my eyes betrayed me by flicking in that direction. Someone, the police perhaps, had placed a large green rug over the area.

Shelby was in her office talking on her cell phone. When I approached, she held up her pointer finger to say she'd be a minute, and I stepped outside the door to give her a privacy. Two clerks were chatting while they worked in the stacks nearby, and I heard the flicking sounds of papers being turned over.

"No, they think it was a robbery." Shelby's voice carried easily through the open doorway.

"Yes, that's what the detective said."

"I don't know."

"I told you I don't know."

"Gotta go. I'll see you tonight, okay?"

"Bye."

Shelby's head popped around the door frame. "Sorry about that, come on in."

Her office was messy; stacks of charts covered most of the surfaces. She cleared off a chair so I could sit, placing the pile of documents on the floor.

Suppressing an urge to tidy the place up, I took a closer look at the files themselves. Every folder had a row of colored tabs along the outside edge, and every tab had a number.

"Why all the colors?" I asked. Our department filed everything by last name; this system was far more complicated.

"It's called terminal digit filing. We file by patient number, starting with the last two digits and moving backwards."

She walked me to the nearest shelf and pointed to the row at eye level. "These charts all end in the number sixty-four. The number sixes are blue, and the fours are green; the colors line up nicely when we've filed them in the right spots."

The files, when lined up, created bands of color; like a horizontal rainbow. "It's kind of pretty."

Shelby smiled. "Well, it's organized; that's why we do it. We're lucky to still be a paper based system. Most hospitals our size have gone to electronic medical records, which would make our department obsolete. We have time to get everyone retrained."

We returned to her office and sat down on opposite sides of her desk. Shelby took a sip from a large white mug with the Holy Heart logo on it, a baby blue cross transposed over a flaming heart.

"It's so weird," she said. "I keep forgetting about what happened to Anna. Just for a few seconds at a time. I can't help but feel like she has a day off, and tomorrow she'll be back like always, humming gospel songs while she works."

Shelby smiled sadly and pulled out a photo from the top drawer of her desk and handed it to me.

"That's Anna and Bridget at our community service day this year."

I looked at Anna's face. Dark brown hair with only a few strands of gray, deep brown eyes, and a smile with a laugh lines around the mouth. There was a smudge of dirt on her cheek, and she was standing next to a freshly dug garden bed, her arm slung over Bridget's shoulders.

"She was a generous person," I said.

"Yes. More like a bossy aunt than an employee sometimes. It's so hard to believe she's not coming back." Shelby stared at a point behind my head, lost in thought. "I'm glad you stopped by the meeting today. I had no idea what to say."

"I was bringing the EAP information, and they snagged me. I didn't expect to see Sally and Bridget there. It was a horrible night, and they were shaken up. Sally, in particular."

"She's tougher than she looks," Shelby said, leaning back in her chair and taking another swallow from her mug. "Sally's our youngest team member, only twenty-eight, but she's been through a lot.

"Her husband died in a car crash three years ago; and she was a stay-at-home mom with no job experience. Her son has a developmental disability, and he requires a lot of care. The accident left them destitute, but the day after her husband's funeral she marched in here to ask for a job.

"She's going to school full time to get her B.A. in Business Administration, which is why she prefers the swing shift."

"Good for her!" I said.

"I agree. Anyway, I have a few questions for you."

"Go for it."

"My team wants to attend the funeral. It'll be hard to coordinate schedules, but I can get a couple of the medical assistants to cover. It might slow us down, but we can make it work. Any problem with that?"

"Not that I can think of. It's your team, so if you've got coverage and your boss is cool with it, who am I to complain?"

Shelby paused. Taking a tip from Detective Patterson's playbook, I waited.

"Kat, are you sure it was a robbery?"

"Nope."

"What! Wait," She rose out of her chair a little. "You told the team—"

"Oh, I have no information to the contrary," I said. "It's an HR thing. You can't make assumptions. So often it looks like one person screwed up, but it wasn't their fault. I prefer to wait for the evidence before making up my mind. There are fewer lawsuits and angry crowds with pitchforks that way."

I smiled, and Shelby relaxed into her chair.

"Why do you ask?"

"If it was a robbery, we can improve our locks. But if it was something else, it might happen again. And that's a problem. I love my work, but no job is worth my life."

"The police are on it, and I don't think they'll let us down," I said. "Speaking of the cops, do you think Anna was using drugs? You saw her every day, and you might have noticed something."

Shelby hesitated. "I never thought she was, or I would have sent her in for a test. No bloodshot eyes, and she was always on time. So, no, I didn't suspect, but..."

"But it's possible, you think?"

"I don't know! The team is adamant she hated drugs, but I never heard her talk about them either way. I didn't think she used them, but how else did the drugs end up in her car?"

"Did anything change for Anna these last few months? Was she nervous, or taking more days off than usual?"

"No, not really. There was a family emergency about a month ago. Something to do with her daughter, Beth. She took off a few days to deal with it."

This didn't seem to square with what the clerks had said. "Is Beth still in the picture? I thought she dropped off the kids and never came back."

Shelby picked up a stress ball off her desk and squeezed it rhythmically. "Anna came to me one morning and said she needed to leave work to file a police report. She said her car was stolen, and she suspected her daughter was behind it.

"She took a couple days off, but didn't bring it up again, and I didn't ask. I try not to get involved in my staff's personal business."

Shelby yawned, and I fought to avoid echoing it. I wondered if she'd gotten any sleep at all after the call from Bridget.

"Other than that, she seemed fine," Shelby said. "She was always a hard worker. Anna took on extra shifts and liked to show off pictures of her grandkids. They started school recently; she talked a lot about that."

I nodded. "Well, I'll let you get back to work. But I'm curious, who were you on the phone with, just now?"

Shelby's cheeks turned pink. "You heard that, huh? I know we aren't supposed to talk to outsiders, but my Mom is worried about me. I made the mistake of telling her about what happened, and now she wants me to get another job."

I was about to commiserate on the topic of bossy mothers, but Shelby was on the move. She picked up a stack of papers from her desk and walked toward the door.

"I gotta get back to work. Thanks a lot for stopping by though. I really mean it."

CHAPTER NINE

I WAS SO DEEP IN thought that I almost collided with Angela.

"There you are. The detective is here. Not the woman, the other one. He's been waiting for fifteen minutes and I've been stalling him."

Angela sounded annoyed, but no more than usual, so I followed her to the conference room without comment. But before she opened the door, she turned to me and said in a low voice, "I want you to note down what he asks and how people respond. And come see me when he's finished."

She entered the room wearing a smile so fake it must have made her face cramp.

"Detective Evans, thank you so much for your patience. Katherine was attending to an urgent matter, but now that she's back, she'll make sure you have whatever you need."

"Thank you," Evans said. "This won't take long."

"We are always happy to help the police," Angela said, waving away his explanation. She closed the doors behind her as she left, leaving me and the detective standing a few feet apart.

"Sorry to keep you waiting," I said.

I remembered him from the previous night. Detective Evans was still in his twenties, but he wore a bushy mustache right out of an eighties cop show. One of my sister Dori's cheesy jokes sprang to mind. *Guns don't kill people. People with mustaches kill people.*

I smothered a smile and invited the detective to take a seat.

"I've only been here a few minutes." He took a seat on one side of the conference room and pulled out a thick spiral bound notepad. "Your boss is a bit of a ball buster, eh?" There was a trace of a Boston accent in his voice.

I relaxed a little. "It has been said. Not by me of course."

"Of course not."

"Will Detective Patterson be joining us?"

"She'd be here, but she had some things she had to do. So, it will just be me today. And you apparently," He didn't seem happy about that last part.

"I'll be as unobtrusive as I can be."

Evans shrugged. He didn't like the arrangement, but he didn't ask me to leave. Score one for Angela.

"Who do you need to talk to?" I asked. He gave me a list. I picked up the phone and dialed.

REAL-LIFE POLICE WORK IS LESS exciting than television had led me to believe. No one slammed their fists on the conference room table, or leaned intimidatingly across the desk. For the most part, we covered the same ground as the prior evening, only in meticulous detail.

Bridget and Sally arrived together and repeated much of what they had said the previous evening. Sally found the body, she screamed, and Bridget came running in right afterward. Bridget performed CPR until the emergency medical technicians arrived.

"There was a cart on the victim when you arrived, is that correct?" Evans asked.

"Yes, it was a file cart. They hold a couple hundred patient charts, and they're heavy," Sally explained. "She might have pulled it on top of herself when she fell back."

"Did anyone else touch the cart?" Evans asked.

"Probably everyone in the department," Bridget said. "We have three carts, and we all share them."

"Can you provide me with a list of everyone who might have touched the cart?"

Bridget nodded and took the pen and paper Evans handed her to write a list of names. Sally checked that list and added a few more. Detective Evans questioned the women on the details of their movements, and their recollections of who was at work that day.

As for me, I was doodling pictures of cats on my notepad. Aside from taking notes for Angela, there was nothing for me to do, and I thought unhappily about all the email messages piling up on my computer.

"Was last night part of your regular shift?" Evans asked.

"For me and Bridget," Sally said. "But not for Anna. She volunteered."

"Under what circumstances did she volunteer?"

"We're doing accreditation prep, and we're behind schedule. Shelby (that's our boss) asked for volunteers to help, and Anna was one of them."

"Who else volunteered for extra work?"

Sally rattled off a few names.

"Did they work last night?"

"No."

"Why not?"

"Shelby lets us pick our shifts, unless there's a problem with coverage," Bridget said.

"You're saying the victim chose to work last night." Evans perked up in his chair.

"I think so," Bridget said. "You'd need to ask Shelby to be sure."

"Had Anna's behavior changed lately? Was she more happy or sad than usual? Or was she missing work?"

"She was in a good mood, but that wasn't unusual," Sally said.

"Did you notice any physical changes, like bloodshot eyes or sloppy dress? Was she more hyper than usual or more relaxed? Or did she seem forgetful?" Evans was describing symptoms of drug abuse, and Sally's eyes narrowed in response.

"No." Her voice was all ice and prickles.

Detective Evans reached into his messenger bag and pulled out a large transparent bag sealed with red tape. Inside was a quart sized plastic bag filled with many smaller bags. The small bags contained white and blue pills, hundreds of them.

"Do you know what this is?" he asked.

"A bag of pills," Bridget said. "Is that what you found in Anna's car?"

Evans leaned forward, excited. "Did she show these to you?"

"No, but her brother told us about your questions," Sally shot back. "He said you think she was selling drugs."

"We found this in Anna's glove compartment. We also found a large sum of cash in her car, and drugs in her purse, including a small quantity of cocaine." He observed the women closely after sharing this information, and I could see he was testing them.

"That is complete bullshit," Sally said. "Anna would never use drugs. Ever."

"Sally," I cautioned. I didn't want her to get combative with the police.

"It can be a shock to find out a friend had a secret," Evans said. "But I need you to think back to the last few weeks and tell me if you remember the victim talking about anyone new in her life. Did she mention a friend by name? Or a meeting? Anything you can tell us will help us find the person who killed her."

"Detective," Bridget began, "it's important you understand why Anna would not do drugs. Do you know about her daughter?"

"Yes, her brother told me about her daughter's drug problems. And sometimes these things run in families." He shrugged.

Bridget spread her hands out flat on the conference room table. "Anna blamed drugs for destroying her family. She always took the subject very seriously. A few years ago, she found out a young man at her church was smoking pot, and she immediately drove him to his parents and insisted they put him in a program. She simply wasn't the kind of person to be involved with drugs. It is impossible."

I watched Bridget as she spoke without any anger and felt the force of her quiet conviction. Detective Evans nodded, but he was glancing out the window where two attractive young women were talking to one another.

He turned to look at Bridget just as I was thinking about kicking him under the table.

"We'll follow up on all credible leads we get. We always follow the evidence to the truth."

"And what if the evidence is fake?" Sally asked.

"I've noted your concerns. Thank you for your cooperation," he said, jotting down notes on his pad of paper. "That's all I need for now."

The women left, and Sally shut the conference room door with more force than was necessary.

Our evening security guards spoke with us, but had seen nothing and heard nothing. They verified there are no security cameras in the basement and there were no previous violent incidents involving Anna Vasquez.

Of the two EMTs on duty the previous evening, neither one was working, but we managed to get one of them on the telephone. His report was all-business.

"We arrived on the scene right at 6:32 p.m. and found one Hispanic female, mid-fifties, unresponsive with what appeared to be two GSW to the chest. We intubated her and began compressions, but she was DOA.

"The medical examiner will need to confirm, but from the amount of bleeding we suspected a torn aorta. She likely bled out in seconds."

"Did you see any indication of who shot her?" Evans asked.

"No. We were focused on the patient, but neither of us saw anyone coming or going."

The last interview of the day was with Robert Chapman, our pharmacy manager. He knocked on the conference room door and pulled over an armless chair that would support his girth before sitting down in it carefully. He pushed his round glasses up higher on his nose and grinned. "This is rather exciting, isn't it?"

I must have stared because he backpedaled. "Not that poor woman being dead, may God rest her soul. I'm sorry; that was insensitive. I meant being part of an official police investigation." He blushed.

Evans flipped his notepad to a fresh sheet of paper. "I understand there was an attempted break-in at the pharmacy. Can you tell me what was missing?"

"According to our initial inventory, nothing's missing. Not a single pill or vial out of place." He used his middle finger to push his glasses higher up on his nose. "I guess they were interrupted before they got inside."

"Can you walk us through what you saw and heard when you arrived at work?" The detective's pen was poised to write.

Robert pulled a cloth handkerchief out of his pocket and mopped his brow.

"I came in early this morning because I saw the email about what happened. Before I left home, I called all our retail shops to make sure everyone was okay. When I got in, I went straight to the storeroom."

"Our hospital has seven retail pharmacy locations," I told the detective. "Patients don't go to the basement location. The basement houses our excess inventory, Robert's office, and a few cubicles for our telephone pharmacists."

"Right," Robert said. "We also do compounding down there. Well, I saw the front door was scratched up. It was locked, but better safe than sorry. We did a complete inventory of the storeroom this morning and everything seems to be in place. We're still inventorying the other locations, but so far nothing is missing."

Detective Evans pulled out the plastic evidence bag again and slid it over in front of Robert. "Do you recognize these?"

Robert smiled and leaned in, his nose just inches from the bag.

"I sure do! I see eighty milligram tablets of Oxycontin; that's some strong stuff there. Ten milligram doses of Adderall. That's a popular street drug for students who want to cram for tests. There are, yes, several dosage sizes of Valium. Those small blue pills there are methylenedioxymethamphetamine, also known as ecstasy. It's quite a haul you've got there."

"Can you tell us if these came from your pharmacy?" Evans asked.

"Technically no, since they're bagged instead of bottled. Once you take a pill out of the bottle, there's no way to identify the source." He pointed at the blue pills and gave me a wink.

"Of course, we don't carry ecstasy here at Holy Heart, although I'm sure it would make our elderly patients sit up taller in their britches."

He laughed, then pushed his glasses back up.

"But no, I don't think these are ours. We'd notice this kind of loss, and besides, do you see these pills here?" He pointed at the white ovals with small numbers stamped on one side.

We nodded.

"They're fakes. Probably manufactured in China. They look almost like the real deal, but whoever takes them is likely to get a dose of placebo, perhaps with a trace of the real stuff mixed in."

Evans thanked Robert for his help. I walked Robert out, and when I returned saw the detective was packed and ready to leave.

"I think we've got what we need here. Thank you for your cooperation."

"What happens next?" I asked. "If someone planted those pills in Anna's car to make her look guilty, shouldn't we—"

His pitying look froze the words in my mouth. "Miss, I can tell you're a nice person, but the world isn't nice. Everyone here wants to believe Ms. Vasquez was a saint, and this was all a big misunderstanding. I see it all the time."

He shifted his weight to one side and heaved his bag over one shoulder.

"I promise we'll check the leads we get. But frankly, the most likely solution is she was mixed up in something big, she got cold feet, and a criminal she was working with shot her.

The best way to find the shooter is to follow the drug money, and that's what we'll do. It's possible the victim was selling here at work. It's more common than you think.

"You can help us by keeping an eye out for any signs of that. Once we find out who her supplier was, we can bring him down."

"But if you talk to more of her friends, you might find—"

The detective's face was a polite mask, but he wasn't hearing me. Still, I had to try. "You may know criminals," I continued, "but I know our employees. Anna wasn't the criminal type. I heard all the same things you did, and it doesn't add up."

"It's nice of you to want to help. But sometimes hunches are wrong." Evans looked at his watch, and I could tell he was ready to leave.

"Yes, hunches can be wrong," I said. I walked him out, and he thanked me for my assistance. I smiled politely and shook his bony hand.

As he strode away, I clenched my fists hard enough to leave fingernail dents in my palms. The police had already made up their minds, but I hadn't.

CHAPTER TEN

AFTER I UPDATED ANGELA, I returned to my office to find a mutiny in progress. Akiko's arms were crossed, and she was standing in front of my door like a human barricade. Her dark eyeliner, pierced nostril, and jet-black hair made her look especially fierce. Our tiny Goth warrior.

"Go home, Kat."

I sighed and shook my head.

"We've got everything under control, and you look like reheated garbage. No offense." She grinned.

She wasn't wrong. I was running on less than four hours sleep and feeling it. On the way back to my office, I had tripped over a chair leg and fallen on all fours onto the carpet. My involuntary screech had caused a job applicant to startle and spill his cup of water all over his resume. Jocelyn helped him print a fresh copy while I bandaged my scuffed knee.

It had been a long day, but I wanted to finish my work before I got even further behind.

"I'm fine, and I have things to do," I protested.

Akiko just stared at me.

"Angela might call," I said.

She didn't budge an inch.

"I've got interviews to do," I whined. "And three manager candidates coming in today."

Jocelyn poked her head over Akiko's shoulder. "If Angela calls, I will forward her to your cell phone. I promise." She handed me my purse and jacket, which she had pulled off the hook in my office without me noticing. "She's right. You need to get some sleep."

"And the interviews?" I asked, defeated but unwilling to admit it.

Akiko shrugged. "I'll take care of them. Email me your notes. I've got all afternoon free. Seriously, if you don't go, I'll have to spend the rest of the day on social media just burning time. I'd be a terrible example to the staff."

Jocelyn nodded solemnly. "I'm very susceptible to a bad example. And I'd end up eating food in public areas, in wild violation of company policy. It would be chaos. You should leave. Before it's too late."

They looked at each other, nodded, and looked back at me.

I was too tired to argue. "I surrender! Fine! I look like crap, and I need a nap."

This rhymed, so I giggled.

The two women looked at each other again, conveying a message I couldn't quite grasp. I emailed Akiko my interview notes and walked to my car.

INVOLUNTARY TURNOVER

Once I was home, I lowered the shades in my bedroom, crawled under the blankets, and fell into oblivion.

WHEN I WOKE UP, IT was pitch black in my room, and Milo was wrapped around the crown of my head like a furry turban. I dislodged him and rolled on my side. The alarm clock read 8:07.

I slipped on my bath robe and slippers and padded into the kitchen with my cell phone pressed against one ear.

> *Hey, Kat, it's Akiko. Just wanted you to know everything went fine today. David liked two of the candidates for his supervisor position, and we're bringing both back for second rounds. I hope you are getting some rest. See ya tomorrow.*
>
> *Katherine, it's your Mom. I haven't heard from you in a while. Call me back.*
>
> *Hey, Kat. It's Dori. Mom says you're not calling her back. The boys are having a game on Saturday, and we're going to barbecue around three. We'd like you to come, too. Bring a friend if you like.*
>
> *Hey there. I'm flying home to Seattle tonight. Want to do takeout tomorrow?*

I smiled at the last message, but didn't bother to try to call Derek back; he was probably already thirty thousand feet in the air. My fingers tapped out a text message instead.

> GOT YOUR MSG. CRAZY WEEK, WILL EXPLAIN LATER. DINNER TOMORROW SOUNDS GOOD. 8:30 MY PLACE?

I picked up my suit jacket off the couch where I had tossed it. It was already covered in a thin veneer of gray-white fur. I had a lint roller in my closet, but the jacket was too far gone. I tossed it into my dry-cleaning bag.

Looking around, I thought my entire condo could use a good going over. I pulled out my cleaning supplies basket and a half dozen freshly laundered hand towels. I plugged in my headset so I could call my mother while I worked.

Nothing makes me feel as relaxed as a newly cleaned condo. The world might be chaos, but my home didn't need to be.

Aggie Voyzey picked up on the third ring.

"You sound miserable," she said, once I'd said hello. "What's going on?"

"Bad week at work, but I'm fine," I said, modulating my voice to a more cheerful tone. "I got your message about the barbecue, and Dori called, too. I'll be there."

"Who the hell barbeques in the middle of the winter in the pouring rain?" she said. "I don't want to freeze my butt off." She paused mid-rant and said, "And of course I'll be there too."

I laughed. "You could stay inside you know. Steve and Dori will do all the cooking, and the rest of us can play board games."

"Yeah. Don't mind me, I'm a bit crabby today," she said. I heard the click of dishes being set down on the counter on the other end of the line.

That reminded me of my task, and I pulled my broom out of the closet and swept the kitchen tiles. Kitty kibble emerged from under the cabinet edges.

"I'm grouchy, too," I said. "We can start a club."

"Been seeing anyone?" she asked.

"I see lots of people every day," I said. If she insisted on quizzing me on my love life, I'd make her work for it.

"Fine Miss Smarty-pants," she said. "Go on any dates lately?"

"Nope," I said. "There's more to life than dating, Mom."

"Sure there is. But romance is part of life too, and it's been long enough, Kat. It's time to get back on the horse. Find yourself a nice stallion and go for a r—"

"Mom!"

Her laughter rang across the line, and I grinned. My mother had been fairly traditional while I was growing up, but retirement was softening her hard edges.

"I'm not trying to nag you, hon. I just want you to be happy again."

"I know. And I'm not unhappy."

"But you're not happy, either."

"It's been a bad week at work. My boss still hates me, and one of our employees was murdered, and I got in trouble for helping someone tone down their tampon costume."

"Say what?"

I filled her in on the last few days.

"Do you think I'm a screw-up?" I asked. It's one of the rules of life that your mother is supposed to be encouraging, and I could use a boost.

"You're not a screw-up, love," she said. "But there's one thing that has been true about you since you were a little girl."

"What's that?"

"You always have to go around fixing everyone else's problems. You can't leave things alone, even when you should."

"That isn't true."

"It is. Remember when Dori told you a boy in her class was bullying her in the second grade?"

I remembered, vaguely. Mostly his smug smile and red hair, and how loud he wailed after I punched him in the nose. Also the sinking feeling of doom while waiting in the principal's office afterward. "Yes. But I was just a kid. I haven't punched anyone in the face since then. Although I've been tempted." I was thinking of a certain mustachioed police officer.

"Hilarious. But you're forgetting the most important part of the story. That boy wasn't really bullying Dori. She was exaggerating, and before you got all the facts straight, you ran up and popped him in the nose.

"You have a lion's heart, Kat, but sometimes you can be naïve. Like you were with the woman in that horrid costume. She dumped her problem on you, and you're the one who got in trouble."

"You think she was trying to go around her supervisor, and she used me as her patsy."

"Yes," my mother said. "And you heard a plausible story and jumped right in and tried to save her."

"I suppose I did." So much for encouraging.

"Tomorrow's another day, Kat. Get some rest and stay out of the terrible business with the murder. Repeat after me: not my problem."

"I love you, Mom."

"Love you, too."

I pulled off my headset and sat it on the kitchen counter so I could kneel and wipe the kitchen floor with a damp cloth.

Was I looking at the murder all wrong? I tried to consider the police's perspective. A woman was shot at work the same night as an attempted robbery of the pharmacy storeroom. The police find drugs and cash in her purse and car. Her daughter has a history of drug abuse, and she has been telling her coworkers for years how terrible drugs are. Perhaps she was just covering?

Something else occurred to me. If Anna's daughter had stolen her car recently, could the daughter have been involved in the murder? She knew where her mom worked, and that there were drugs nearby. She had access to the car. Maybe she tried to distract her mother while her friends broke into the pharmacy?

I might not share Sally's certainty that Anna was being framed, but I agreed with her on one thing. The truth should come out even if it wasn't easy or comfortable.

It couldn't hurt to ask a few questions, to alleviate the concerns of Anna's friends and my own conscience. In work and in life, justice should always prevail.

CHAPTER ELEVEN

YOU KNOW THAT FEELING IN your gut when you've made a terrible mistake? And the way it twists your stomach like a balloon animal? Yeah, me too.

Erin showed up at my office while our new hires were on a coffee break. She runs new hire orientation, and we had a group of nine that day.

"You need to see this." She thrust a sheet of paper at me; it was a standard Washington State Patrol background check, the kind we run on every new hire. Because medical staff work with vulnerable groups, like children, the elderly, and people under anesthesia, we can't hire anyone with a criminal history.

The page had one name listed: Priscilla Mann. And there were two felony convictions on her record. One for arson and another for assaulting a police officer.

"Whoa," I said.

"Yeah, whoa indeed. What should I do with her?"

"She's here? Now? You're telling me we hired her?"

"Yes, she's at orientation chatting up a storm with the new cardiologist. The offer went out yesterday afternoon, so we're playing catch up on paperwork. This just came back today." Erin placed one hand her hip and cocked her head at me expectantly.

"Did we screw up?" I watched my career flash past my eyes. If we'd let someone start without a background check, my ass was grass.

"Nope. David Cobb signed off on an expedited start date."

My stomach stopped doing somersaults; this wasn't our fault. Managers are supposed to give HR three days' notice before starting a new hire, so we can take care of the details. You know, the little things like ordering them a password from IT and making sure they're not a convicted arsonist.

One of our executives granted an exception to our rule, and there we were, wondering how many fire extinguishers were in the building.

"What is she like?" I had a hard time envisioning an arsonist drinking coffee in our conference room. I had an even harder time imagining how to handle the conversation. *Hello, ma'am? I understand you torched a building once. Can we have a chat outside, away from all the combustible materials?*

Erin shrugged. "She's nice enough, and she's not carrying a blowtorch if that's what you're worrying about." Erin smirked at my discomfort. Giving employees bad news isn't part of her job, and she knew it. "They'll be back from the coffee break in five minutes."

"Give me a minute to organize my thoughts, then bring her in here. I'll let her go."

"I'll have a hose on standby."

PRISCILLA WAS FIVE-FOOT-FOUR WITH BLUE eyes, medium brown hair that brushed her shoulders and a polite smile. She looked more like a middle school teacher than someone who had done time for setting fires.

"Hi, Priscilla, I'm Kat, the HR Director."

"It's nice to meet you." She shook my hand and took a seat.

"I asked to see you because we received your background check today."

Pausing mid-sentence is a great way to size a person up. I looked for any sign she was exploding with rage, but instead she heaved a small sigh.

"And unfortunately I need to withdraw your offer because of your recent felony convictions."

Priscilla nodded at this, but didn't respond.

"Normally we run our background checks prior to hire, but because you were hired so fast, there was a short delay. I'm very sorry about that. Because this was our mistake, we'll pay you for both days of orientation even though you'll be going home now."

"Thank you," she responded. "I knew there was a risk I wouldn't be hired, but I was hoping I squeaked by, or that you guys didn't background check."

"Hospitals are required by law to conduct background checks," I explained. "Sometimes if a conviction is very old or very minor, we can get an exception, but I'm afraid in this case it isn't possible."

Priscilla smiled warmly. "You're being very nice about all this, and I appreciate it. Arson sounds like a big deal, but my case was different."

I wondered what the folks at Washington State Corrections would say to this.

"You're skeptical, and that's okay. Two years ago, my husband left me right after he blew through our life savings. Turns out he was supporting a mistress on the side, and they had a baby." Priscilla spoke calmly, almost as if she was describing someone else's life. "They were renting a house together, and I dumped all of his belongings on the front lawn and lit them on fire." She blushed. "Not my best move, I know. Unfortunately, there was oil on the ground from a car that had been towed, and the fire spread to the neighbor's porch. No one was hurt, thank God. I did um—smack the police officer when he tried to cuff me. It wasn't my best day."

Having been through a bad breakup myself, I could empathize with her desire to douse the bastard's tighty whities in gasoline.

"I'm so sorry you had to go through all that," I said. "It sounds like hell."

She shrugged and picked up her purse to sit it in her lap. "I screwed up. Fire is dangerous! I had to serve three months, but I met these great women up in Purdy. Made some lifelong friends. And the plus side is that if Jack saw me walking up the street, he'd hop in the nearest car and drive the other direction."

I laughed. I bet he would!

"Unfortunately, I still have to withdraw your offer," I said, hoping she realized that her story didn't negate the decision.

"I expected so. Can I say goodbye to the rest of the orientation group? I'll tell them my daughter called and needs me to pick her up early from school. Wouldn't want to shock them."

"Of course," I said, and then added in a few words of advice. "Your criminal history will make it harder for you to find a job, but you'll have better luck applying to small companies and family owned shops. Also, check out warehouse and manufacturing businesses. They're less squeamish and may give you a fair hearing. Good luck, Priscilla."

She flashed me a smile and dropped off her brand new name badge at my desk. I'd done my job. And I hoped Priscilla would find someone who would let her do hers too.

AFTER I FIRED PRISCILLA, I got two email messages simultaneously. One was from Sally, and the second was from Angela. They both wanted to see me right away, but in the case of a tie, victory goes to the person who approves your paychecks.

I entered the executive suite and told the admin at the front desk I was there to see Angela. She said I should sit, but instead I wandered over to the wall where our company awards are displayed. Our *Best Places to Work* trophy was six years old and covered in a thin layer of dust. I pulled a tissue from a nearby box and wiped the dust away.

"She's ready to see you now," she said. I stood taller and tried to walk into my boss's office with something approximating confidence. I wasn't going to let her psych me out this time.

Fortunately for me, Angela was in a good mood, by which I mean she didn't glare at me or point out a mistake I had made.

"Take a seat, Katherine. I want your opinion." Angela hit the button on her phone that sends all calls to voicemail.

She wanted my opinion? She didn't want to be interrupted? I wasn't sure if I should be flattered or afraid.

"Have you met the dead woman's family yet?" she asked.

"No. We sent a floral arrangement, and we're preparing benefits information for her next of kin. Why?"

"I'm concerned they may bring a suit against us." Angela leaned back in her chair and tented her fingers.

"Why would they sue us?"

"Why wouldn't they?" Angela looked at me blankly. "It's what people do when they're angry. We'd win, because she was found with drugs and probably brought this on herself, but I'd like to avoid a legal conflict if at all possible. Perhaps offer a settlement preemptively."

I bit back an irritated response, and said "I'm not sure they'd sue us, just to get a payday."

"I hope you're right," she said. "But you don't have as much experience as I do, and trust me, when a tragedy occurs, after the dust settles everyone looks for someone to blame. If they don't blame her, we're the next logical target."

As much as I didn't want to embrace Angela's low opinion of humanity, a small part of me acknowledged that she might be right. We didn't know how the family would react.

"I want you to meet them," Angela said. "Take the benefits information you were going to mail and deliver it in person. See if you can feel them out. And let's give them something to ease any hard feelings. I've talked to Gary, and he agrees we'll pay Anna's dependents' medical expenses for one year. He wrote a letter explaining this. Give it to them." Angela slid a manila envelope across the desk to me.

"I'm glad to talk to them," I said, "but I don't like the idea of trying to buy them off like this. Can't we pay for the COBRA because it's the right thing to do?"

"Whatever reason you want to give them is fine. Certainly, the concerns about a lawsuit should stay between you and me."

She paused for a moment. "Katherine—this may sound harsh, but if your goal is to advance your career, you need to ditch some of your Pollyanna attitude. People can be vindictive, especially when they're hurting. And we have an obligation to protect this hospital from those who would attack it. It's common sense.

"Besides, if our employees are dealing drugs underneath our noses, we could use more suspicion from HR, not less." Her tone softened. "Something to think about."

I wasn't sure how to respond. Angela and I didn't see eye to eye on much (and this was no exception), but for once she was trying to give me advice.

"I'll call the Vasquez family today and see when I can come by to meet them. And I'll tell you if I detect any signs they blame us for what happened."

"Good," she said. "I'd also like you to go to the funeral as a representative of Holy Heart."

"I hate funerals. Besides, Shelby and her crew are already going."

"Then you'll fit right in. Keep me posted."

CHAPTER TWELVE

I RETURNED SALLY'S CALL WHEN I got back to my office, and she picked up on the first ring.

"Hey, I got your message. I'm about to go get lunch; can we meet this afternoon?"

"Are you eating in the cafeteria? I'll meet you there, if that's okay." Sally sounded eager, even happy. I was hoping for a quiet meal, but I didn't want to leave her hanging.

"Sure. Are you sure you wouldn't rather meet in my office?"

"No. There's someone I want you to talk to. We'll see you in ten minutes."

"Can you give me a hint about what this is about?"

"It's about Anna." She hung up, leaving me holding the receiver in the air.

Our cafeteria is shared by both patients and staff. It's bordered on two sides by deli-style counters where you can fill up your plate with heart clogging fried foods (quite popular) or a salad bar (less popular).

INVOLUNTARY TURNOVER 81

Our doctors may not smoke, at least not on-site, but they are not above slamming a couple double cheeseburgers between rounds. A cynical person might say we're on both the supply and demand side of the healthcare business.

I bought a sandwich and a cookie and surveyed the room for Sally. She arrived a moment later with a guy in his early twenties that looked faintly familiar. Sally greeted me and walked us back to a table in the corner.

I could tell right away that Sally's friend wasn't happy to be there. I sipped my tea and let her take the lead.

Sally introduced us. "Matt, this is Kat from HR. You can trust her."

This was high praise, but I was puzzled. Was Matt an employee? He wasn't wearing a name badge, but I was certain I had seen him before somewhere.

"Matt is a pharmacy tech. He has something to say, but he doesn't want to get in trouble."

Classic, I thought. Someone wants to confess something to me, but forbids me from doing or saying anything about it. It's the human resources' curse.

"Is this about the murder?" I asked.

Sally nodded. "The police think Anna was killed because she interrupted a robbery and was involved in it somehow, right?"

"That's the theory."

"But it wasn't a robbery," she said triumphantly. "And now we have proof!"

"Matt, do you know who shot her?" My heartbeat quickened.

"No way!" He held his hands out defensively in front of himself. "I wasn't even there. My shift ends at five-thirty."

I waited for him to explain, but he looked down at the table.

Sally fixed Matt with an expectant look, but he wouldn't meet her gaze.

"He doesn't want to get fired," she said to me.

If he felt safer, he might spill the beans, but I had to be careful about what I promised. "Matt, there are certain things I'm required to report when I hear them. Like someone hurting someone else, someone being harassed or threatened, or anything that means a patient might be hurt."

He nodded.

"If you saw something important, I want you to tell me. I promise I will do my best to keep you from getting in trouble."

"See, I told you," Sally said.

I hoped she wouldn't have to eat those words.

"Okay," Matt sighed and placed his hands flat on the table. "The police said Anna was shot during a robbery, but that doesn't make any sense."

"Why not?" I asked. "Someone tried to break into the pharmacy at the same time."

"But nothing was stolen." Matt insisted. "All the opiates and drugs with street value were left alone. Not one pill out of place."

"They tried to break the lock with a crowbar, but it didn't give," I said. "Anna probably interrupted them before they could finish, or they fled when they heard the gunshot."

His ears flushed a dark red, and he mumbled something too low to hear.

"What?" I asked, leaning in.

"The door wasn't even locked," he muttered.

"What?"

"He forgot to lock the door," Sally whispered.

He nodded and looked around, miserable. No wonder he was afraid to come forward. If Robert found out about this, he'd be fired on the spot. Leaving all those drugs accessible was an immensely dumb mistake, especially for a pharmacy employee who knew better.

"I can't believe I was so stupid," he said, echoing my thoughts. "We had a delivery in the afternoon, and I meant to re-lock the door. I woke up at like four a.m. and realized what I'd done. I came back and locked up."

"You didn't do it on purpose," Sally said. "And no drugs were taken."

"What if someone took something? They could have died. We keep dangerous medicines in there." He hung his head.

"See, Kat?" Sally said, "it wasn't a robbery. If they wanted the drugs, they could have walked in and taken them. Why the big show about trying to force the door open?"

"Criminals aren't known for their smarts," I said. "Is it possible they assumed the door was locked?"

Matt shook his head again. "Nah, it swings open real easy. If they tried to pry it open at all, it would have popped open. There's no way they didn't know."

"Then why didn't the police notice the door was unlocked?" I asked.

He shrugged.

"But even if the door was unlocked, Anna still might have interrupted the crime," I said. "I'm not sure what this changes."

"It matters because why would you use a crowbar to scrape up an open door?" Sally asked. "They could step inside and steal without anyone seeing. It's like whoever did this was trying too hard to make her look guilty. This was a frame job."

The pharmacy technician cradled his head in his hands and moaned. "I cannot afford to lose this job. No one else will ever hire me again. And I still owe on my student loans."

"The police need to know they're on the wrong track," Sally said.

Matt wasn't listening. He rubbed his forehead with one hand. "If I tell Robert, he'll fire me." His face blanched. "My mother is going to kill me."

I hid a smile. Matt was at least twenty-five, but his apron strings were still firmly attached.

"Give me a minute," I said, pausing for a few bites of my sandwich. I weighed our options to find the one that would cause the least harm.

"Here's what I think. You should have told Robert about this." Matt sank into his chair even further. "Nothing was taken, though, and you did the right thing today by telling the truth." I left out the part where his coworker dragged him to see me.

Two pairs of eyes watched me while my heart weighed the ethics of the situation. The balance tipped to one side, and I could only hope I was right.

"It's the police that need this information, right?"

Matt nodded, and Sally looked relieved.

"I'll call them and tell them about the unlocked door. I won't bring up your name unless they ask, and I won't tell Robert. Is that fair?"

Matt exhaled. "Thank you."

"I have two conditions," I added. "One, that you promise never to make this mistake again. Ever."

He nodded emphatically. "I promise."

"Second, when I get fired for not reporting this, you both help me find a new job." I said this last bit sarcastically, but they both nodded as if taking an oath.

"We've got your back," Sally said.

"I know you do. I'll call the police tonight and tell you what they say. Check back with me on Monday."

Matt left, walking like a man given a reprieve, but I asked Sally to stay.

"I've been wondering. Do you think Beth could have been involved in this?"

She pursed her lips, then nodded. "Totally."

CHAPTER THIRTEEN

BACK AT HOME, I POWERED through the pain. My knees were getting bruised from the hardwood, but I was determined to scrub every square inch of my living room floor.

My brief conversation with Detective Evans had left me unsatisfied, and I was taking my anger out on the dirt hiding beneath my area rug. The physicality of moving furniture and the sensation of grinding the scrub-brush into the floor felt satisfying.

I slid back my cream-colored sofa and exposed a nest of cat hair dust bunnies and a deep burgundy tie with golden flecks in it.

As my hand closed around the tie, I remembered the night I playfully removed it from Neil's neck before undoing the buttons of his starched white shirt. A familiar mix of regret and bitterness rose up to sting my heart; I tossed the tie to one side where Milo pounced on it.

It had been almost a year since Neil had moved out. We'd dated for two years, lived together for one, and my cup of happiness was full when he proposed last fall.

Unfortunately, the engagement ring came with strings attached. And when I balked at his demands, he walked out.

After the initial shock of being dumped had faded, I found myself enjoying the single life. No more cooking meals the way he liked them. And no more negotiating over how to spend our time off. I had twice the closet space, and I never needed to share the TV remote or kick Milo out of bed to appease him.

Fortunately, I had insisted on purchasing the condo in my own name, declining to put him on the deed until we were actually wed. He may have left, but I still had my home.

At less than eight hundred square feet, my condo is small, but to me it's perfect. Perched on Harvard Avenue at the crest of Seattle's Capitol Hill neighborhood, I've got a view of the city lights from my bedroom window. The hum of activity on the street below provides comforting background noise, the urban equivalent of birdsong or wind chimes.

Capitol Hill is known as Seattle's gay and lesbian district, but to me it has always been a cheerful mishmash of humanity. Corporate yuppies, skateboarding teens, elderly couples holding hands, and sharply dressed locals all walk the same streets and eat the same greasy burgers under the bright lights at Dick's Drive In.

I wasn't ready to date, and I didn't know if I'd ever be. Friendship was more my speed because friends don't try to change you. And as for the rest, well, Babes in Toyland is just a short stroll from my condo.

When my doorbell rang, I got up and brushed off my knees.

I MET DEREK ONE MONTH after Neil moved out.

My cousin was getting married, and I was dreading the rehearsal dinner. I could still see the dent on my finger where my engagement ring had once been (in Seattle, there are no tan lines), and smiling at cousin Sue's wedded bliss sounded as fun as a fork in the eye. But we're family, and that means something to me, so I went.

We were at Bucca de Beppo, sitting around the table of honor—the one with the plaster head of the pope sitting in the middle—when a stranger sat next to me and introduced himself as "Derek, a friend of your sister's."

When I saw Dori eating pasta across from me with an all-too-innocent look, I almost walked out. I was newly single, grieving, and she was shoving eligible men under my nose.

Surprisingly, Derek and I discovered that we liked each other. Not in a screw-like-bunnies way, but in a good-buddies kind of way. Between dinner and dessert, we made a deal. He'd accompany me to Sue's wedding to get my relatives to shut up, and I'd return the favor and accompany him to one of his obligatory family gatherings.

He hasn't called in his side of the bargain yet, but we've been friends ever since.

I opened the door to find Derek bearing a box of red wine in one hand and balancing a stack of takeout cartons on his opposite arm.

"Didn't they give you a bag?" I asked.

"Have you learned nothing from me?" Derek is an environmentalist, but he doesn't get too uppity about it.

"What's with the wine? Are we celebrating?" I took a couple of the cartons from him before he dropped them on my newly cleaned floor.

"Yes. We are celebrating the former Mr. and Mrs. Jacobson who are successfully unmarried after many rounds of fruitful negotiation."

Derek is a professional mediator specializing in divorces. After a few years litigating, he decided that the courts were the wrong place to dissolve a marriage and started his own mediation business focusing on collaborative divorce.

"Mazel tov to the divorcees! Another marriage cheerfully imploded!" I called, raising the carton of wine aloft. I placed the boxes on the coffee table and went into the kitchen to get wine glasses and plates. Derek was already rummaging in my silverware drawer.

"You make fun of my job, but you know I'm on the side of goodness and light." He carried the plates and forks into the living room. I followed with the glasses.

I sat down in my comfortable green chair and Derek sprawled out on the couch. Milo walked across his thighs, purring loudly, no doubt puncturing his expensive slacks.

"Milo!" I said. "Off the furniture!" The cat shot me a look of deep contempt but obeyed, lying on the rug beneath the glass coffee table to watch the food from below.

"Sure, you do good work. But I have a hard time seeing divorce as a positive. Most of your clients have kids. How is breaking up families beneficial?"

He handed me a plate and nudged a carton of pad thai closer to me.

"You believe people should stay in relationships forever, even when they're miserable?" This was an old argument between us, but I wouldn't let him off without a fight. I'd learned something about lawyers: No matter how "collaborative" they are, they enjoy a verbal battle.

"No, but people shouldn't have kids unless they're able to stay together." I argued. "Why build a house on a rotten foundation?"

"Sometimes the foundation is good, and a meteor comes through the roof," he grinned.

"Excuses, excuses." I'd seen my parents' ugly divorce before my father's death, and I'd watched Dori and her husband support one another over the years through difficult times. Marriage was a choice, and once you made that choice, you needed to honor it. Unless someone was abusive. That was different.

"People change," Derek said around a mouthful of panang curry. "Most marriages can adapt, but sometimes it's too much. When that happens, it's my job to help everyone move on, feeling respected and cared for instead of torn apart. It's possible to have a good breakup, you know."

"I don't see it, but I'll have to take your word for it."

"Well, then what's new in your world? You said your week was craaaazy." He pantomimed flailing his hands in terror. "And it smells like lemon Pledge in here. Have you been stress-cleaning again?"

"An employee died on Thursday. Was murdered actually. At work."

I watched his eyebrows lift upward in increments as he took in each bit of data.

"That's terrible. Did they catch who did it? Was anyone else hurt?"

I shook my head and gave him the rundown of the last few days, ending with my call to the police department that afternoon.

"When you told him about the unlocked door, what did he say?" Derek asked.

"He said he'd pass it along to Detective Patterson." Not that I believed him. I may as well have called him to tell him it was raining.

"You sound annoyed. But isn't passing it along what you wanted him to do?"

"Yes, but it was the way he said it. Like I had wasted his time by calling. Like I was a crazy person calling to complain about the voices in my head. I told him I'd appreciate it if he would do his frigging job and investigate."

Derek grinned. "I'm sure he loved that."

"I don't care! A woman is dead. Is it too much to ask to have someone give a damn?"

He leaned back against the couch cushions and let Milo settle onto his lap. "I'm surprised is all. It's not like you to argue with authority figures. You're a go with the flow type." I must have bristled at this because he kept going. "No, it's not a bad thing. It's good that you respect authority but you're usually more strategic about what you say. I'm just trying to imagine the guy's reaction."

"The police are used to dealing with hysterical relatives and friends," I said. "I doubt I'm even one of the top five angry people he talked to today."

"Right. But you barely knew this woman. Why are you taking it so personally?"

I went to look out the window. "Isn't it obvious? One of our people was murdered at work!" I turned to Derek and waited for a reaction, but he shrugged.

"The police say it was a robbery attempt even though that doesn't make sense. One of us is dead, her family and friends are mourning, and everyone is expecting them to accept it and move on. 'Your friend, your grandmother, your coworker—she was just a drug dealer, so she deserved what she got.'"

"Is that what they said?" he asked.

"Close enough. My point is that no one who should give a shit does. They're all like 'la-dee-dah, it's so sad,' let's get back to work. Ugh!"

I returned to my food and stabbed a piece of tofu, twice.

"Feel better?"

"A little."

He pointed to the tofu. "You killed it. Now you have to eat it. It's nature's law."

I took a few bites and poured more wine into our glasses.

"You're upset people are moving on. What do you think they should be doing?"

"Finding the murderer. Taking names. Kicking ass. Asking questions. Measuring shit and snapping photos. You know, all the stuff they do on CSI."

"You'll feel better if someone takes action," he repeated back. He was using his mediator mind-tricks on me, but I let it slide.

"Exactly. We owe it to Anna."

"We?" he said.

"The company. She came to work and got killed. It's not our fault, but when it happens on our turf, we're responsible! We need to make sure it never happens again."

"And what if it was a random event?" he said. "I'm not saying it was, but isn't there a chance the police are right? Or perhaps they're still investigating, but not advertising that fact."

I sipped the wine, "Maybe. But I can't sit back and have faith that other people will do the right thing. Faith is for chumps."

As I said this last bit, I wondered if I had had too much wine, but Derek just laughed.

"I like that. You should put it on a bumper sticker." He carried a dirty dish into the kitchen and placed it in the dishwasher. "Then what's the answer, if waiting around and having faith isn't good enough, Kat? Are you going to solve this murder yourself?"

"Why not? I investigate things all the time at work. Besides, I have the perfect excuse to do some digging." I told him about my plan to visit the Vasquez family on Monday. "Angela practically gave me her blessing."

"Just promise me you won't get in trouble."

"Me? Never."

"If you get arrested, at least you have an outstanding lawyer." He puffed out his chest and flexed his arms, bodybuilder style.

"Mediator," I said.

He stuck his tongue out at me.

"Thanks, by the way," I said as I flopped back down on the couch.

"For what?" he asked, stroking Milo's fur.

"The usual. Listening to me complain. Bringing Thai food. Being you."

Derek smiled. "Anytime." He pulled Milo into his lap and asked, "Are the police okay with you asking questions about the crime?"

"There's nothing illegal about asking questions."

"True, but—"

"I'll treat it like any other workplace investigation. You interview the witnesses, ask them what they saw, keep good notes, try to gather the facts. Wait for the truth to emerge."

Derek was shaking his head. "I see. You're going to walk up to people and say, 'Where were you on the night of October 31st?'"

I shrugged. "Well, it works on *Law and Order*, but I can be subtle. Do you have a better idea?"

"Perhaps," he said. "When people don't want to talk, I find it helpful to look for the truth behind the small things."

"The small things?"

"Yes. Like Mr. and Mrs. Jacobson, my new divorcees. They were both nice people, but the whole process fell apart when Mrs. Jacobson would not share custody of the family dog. Everything else was falling in line, but that dog was the sticking point. They were both adamant about getting canine custody."

"Perhaps they really loved the dog."

"No, the wife hated the dog. She called him the poopinator."

"Funny. Perhaps she was keeping the dog out of spite then, to get back at her husband."

"That's what he thought. But I knew I couldn't come right out and ask about the dog because it had become such a hot-button issue. Neither one would give an inch and talking about who should get the dog made everyone clam up."

"How did you get her to give up the dog?"

"I didn't," he said with a smug expression.

"She kept it?"

"No. What I'm saying is that no one could 'make her' give up the dog. She had to decide for herself."

"Okay, so how did you accomplish that?"

"I'm very proud of this one—"

"I can tell; pretty soon we'll need to order you larger hats."

"We had to talk about the dog without talking about the dog, if you know what I mean."

"I don't."

"I asked her what she was worried about in the divorce, and what was most important to her. She didn't talk about the dog at all, but she did talk about her son. He's fifteen, and it turns out he really loves that animal. She believed if her husband got the dog, she'd never see her son."

"Wow," I said.

"I know, right? That's my point. You can't ask the direct question. It's too scary. You need to question people about their feelings, and the truth will come out at you, but usually sideways."

"You think I should ask about people's feelings, not the murder itself."

"It's worth a try."

"And I should probably stop yelling at the cops."

"Not a bad idea either."

"You're good at this, Mr. Stevenson. How did you learn all this stuff?"

"Why, ma'am," he said with a fake southern drawl, "I'd answer that question, but I wouldn't want to get too big for my hats."

CHAPTER FOURTEEN

I SHOULD HAVE BEEN PREPARED to see Neil again, but after he'd moved to Ballard with a buddy of his, I assumed he'd stay off the hill. When you dump a girl like a sack of garbage, it's only fair to cede some territory in the process. Those were the rules. Everyone knew it.

Dori's barbecue was less than an hour away, and I was trying to find something I could pass off as home cooking. I subsisted on a mixture of Thai food and takeout salads from Whole Foods, which is why my fridge contained one lump of cheese, half of a wilted Caesar salad, and one can of diet soda still attached to the plastic rings from the six pack.

I was in the deli at QFC choosing between two types of pasta when I heard a familiar voice one aisle over.

"You pick. It doesn't matter to me," Neil said.

"Chocolate then," a woman's voice replied.

I froze in place. Neil thought chocolate was boring, a fact he never failed to remind me of if I dared bring a pint of Chunky Monkey home on a Friday night.

"That sounds great," Neil said, his voice carrying easily over the divider. My heart sped up a little. Why was my body responding like I still liked him? Old habits die hard, I thought.

I felt exposed, so I walked around the back of the store, away from the voices, to hide next to the magazine aisle.

The last thing I wanted was to get caught making insincere small talk, so I pulled a magazine off the rack at random and turned protectively to one side, hoping he would slide right by.

No such luck, the voice was getting closer. Perhaps I'd go to the ice cream aisle. They'd already been there, so it seemed safe.

"Kat, is that you?" He was right next to me. *Shit.*

I lowered the magazine and smiled; my face felt like molded plastic. "It sure is. How have you been doing?"

"Really well! Just doing a little shopping on the way to Amanda's parents' house for dinner. Kat, this is Amanda."

She stepped out from behind him. All of her. Pregnant enough to pop, with a big silly grin on her face. Neil had a matching smile, and my heart collapsed like a black hole.

"It's so nice to meet you," she extended a manicured hand for me to shake. "Neil has told me all about you."

I wanted to decline, citing the risk of cooties, but I shook her hand anyway and lied through my smiling teeth.

"It is nice to meet you."

The three of us stood there for a moment, but my fight-or-flight response was screaming 'flight'.

"Anyway, I just stopped in for a magazine," I said, holding it up briefly. "Have a nice day."

Have a nice day? That's the best I could do? No matter, they were behind me and out of sight.

To save face, I walked up to the register and paid for the magazine. It wasn't until I took the receipt from the cashier that I looked at it.

Double Shit.

It rained on me the entire way back to my car. It wasn't until I'd turned on the ignition that I realized I'd forgotten to buy any food.

AT DORI'S HOUSE, ABOUT AN hour later, my sister sipped her beer and waited for the end of my story.

"And that's when I saw I was holding a copy *Mature Pregnancy* magazine," I said.

Dori's look of sisterly concern twisted a little, her mouth twitched, and then she flung back her head and laughed so hard that tears sprang from her eyes. She wiped them with one sleeve and reached over to hug me. "Sorry, Kat. I'm not laughing at you, just the situation."

"I know, sis. If it wasn't me, I'd laugh too." We were standing under the eave on her back porch trying to stay dry while we watched the burgers sizzle on her gas barbecue. Dori's two boys were chasing each other in the backyard, oblivious to the rain and mud.

"Mom," her youngest called out, "I'm hungry."

"Ten minutes! Go inside and leave your muddy boots on the porch. Ask daddy to find you some dry clothes. And take your brother."

Michael and Justin are seven-year-old twins. They both have blond hair like my brother-in-law Steve, but they've inherited the mossy green eyes from the Voyzey clan. They're good kids, unless they are tired and cranky, which seems to be the best you can expect with young children.

Her parental duties discharged for the moment, Dori turned her attention back to me. "Seriously, are you okay?"

"Sure. I was startled to see him is all."

Dori went to the grill and inspected the burgers. "His girlfriend was pregnant Kat. How could you be okay with that?"

I crossed my arms over my stomach and leaned back against the siding. It felt cold and rough against my unprotected neck. "It makes total sense. He wanted a baby; I didn't. Why shouldn't he go knock up the next woman he sees?"

"Weren't you jealous?" Dori asked quietly. "I would have been."

Jealousy was the last thing on my mind, but I could see how Dori might see it that way. To her, motherhood was the ultimate vocation.

"Not. I'm hurt he broke up with me, and sad about the whole thing. But mostly I'm angry he threw us away on a whim because I wouldn't let him impregnate me on his time table."

"I liked Neil, but he was a control freak," Dori said.

That was true. He had to have his shirts hung up in a certain way, his steak cooked to a particular standard. I'd never realized how much I'd shaped myself to his whims until he was gone.

"I put up with his quirks for two years, and he can't even give us six months to sort out the kid issue. It's like he held our entire relationship hostage. Hand over your birth control pills, or I'll shoot."

Dori walked up to me and put her arm around my shoulders. "I'm sorry sis. I'd hoped he was the one for you."

"Me, too," I said, hugging her back. "I should be grateful, really. Amanda can have him and his quirks. I don't think I want to be a mother, and perhaps that meant we were doomed from the start."

"Perhaps," she said. She looked through the sliding glass door and into the kitchen where her husband was tying Justin's shoelaces. She beamed at them and then gave me a look that was more pitying than sympathetic. Dori would always pity me, I realized. And somehow that made me even sadder than seeing Neil at the corner store.

"Enough moping," Dori said. She quickly slid the burgers off the grill and pointed at the kitchen with one foot. "Let's go in and I'll make you cocoa, and you can tell me all about what's new with you."

My mother arrived just as we were setting the table. She sat a bowl of her famous (to us at least) potato salad on the kitchen counter.

"How are my little men?" she called out. The two boys went flying into her arms as she knelt down.

"Take this bowl into the kitchen and give it to your daddy." She handed the large plastic bowl to the boys, who managed to carry it tandem without dropping it on the carpet.

"They're getting so big!" she said to Dori. She stripped off her wet wool jacket and laid it over one arm of the living room sofa.

My mother surveyed me with a critical eye and then embraced me. "You look tired. You've been working too much, haven't you, because of the murder?" She reached up and untangled a few locks of my hair with her fingers.

"I'm fine," I said. "How are you doing? And where's Bob?" Bob is my mother's latest boyfriend. She seemed to go through about one a year, and as such rarely brings them to family gatherings. She draws a firm line between her social life and her family life. Not that the rest of us are permitted that luxury.

"What murder?" Dori asked.

"Some Mexican woman was dealing drugs at the hospital and got gunned down. A very sad story," my mother said.

"Jesus, Mom. Anna is Latina, not Mexican. And we don't know if she was dealing drugs. It's not like she deserved this. She left two grandchildren behind."

My mother shrugged. "Mexican, Latina, whatever. It's a description, not an indictment. And besides, didn't you say they found pills in her car?"

"The police are looking into it. It's possible her daughter may have been involved. I'm—I mean they're—still investigating."

The boys ran back into the living room to show Mom their latest toys, something about dinosaurs that fly, and Dori shot me a look to say we'd discuss this later, when the kids were in bed.

We never did get a chance to talk. After dinner we'd played a game of Go Fish, and Justin had beaten us all handily. It was a good thing we were playing for chocolate chips, or else he might have cleaned out my bank account. I was home by eight, bearing a tray of leftovers and with most of the melancholy lifted from my heart.

CHAPTER FIFTEEN

ANY ANXIETY I FELT ABOUT visiting the Vasquez family melted away when I talked to Thomas Vasquez on the phone. He said he was eager to meet me and invited me to come by for tea.

While I felt guilty about spying on them for Angela, I was curious what they'd heard from the police, and if they'd considered the possibility that Anna's daughter, Beth, might be involved in her murder.

My first stop of the day was Davis's desk. He was frowning at his computer screen when I arrived, but he smiled and looked up when I knocked on his door frame.

"Good morning. I'm going to visit Anna's family today. I'd like to present them with information on continuation of benefits. Can you help me put a packet together?"

"It's already done; I planned to deliver it by courier this afternoon."

"I'd like to do it in person. To pay our respects to the family."

He smiled. "That's good of you. Would you like me to come? I might be able to answer questions for them."

"You'd go with me?" I asked, surprised.

"Sure. I think it's important we honor our employees and their families. I want Anna's family to know we still care about them." He brushed invisible lint off his sweater. "Besides, I'm the benefits expert. You might say the wrong thing and ruin my perfect record." He laughed.

"We wouldn't want that."

David handed me a heavy manila envelope with a clasp enclosure. I took a moment to familiarize myself with its contents.

On the top was Davis's summary, describing what Anna's family was entitled to. Her retirement account contained approximately forty thousand dollars, and her brother Thomas was the beneficiary. Her final paycheck, accrued vacation, and sick leave totaled thirty-five hundred dollars, and the check was enclosed.

Beneath the summary, there was a letter from our CEO explaining that the company would pay for Anna's family's health premiums for a full twelve months.

"I know we didn't have to do it, but I'm glad we did," Davis said.

The cynical part of my brain piped up with the comment that the company was just trying to stave off a wrongful death lawsuit, but I kept that to myself.

"I'm glad we did it, too," I said.

Beneath the stack of benefits forms, there were six letters of appreciation for Anna and two company service awards.

"Were these from her employee file?"

"Yeah. It was Jocelyn's idea. She thought the family might want them."

"No life insurance though?"

"No, she canceled her coverage a few months ago. If I remember correctly, she found a better deal through a broker."

The only other item in the packet was a sympathy card, signed by everyone in HR. Davis handed me a pen to add my name.

"This is beautiful work," I said. "Let's go share it."

THOMAS VASQUEZ WAS A BEAR of a man who bore little resemblance to his sister, except that they shared the same broad smile and dark hair. He welcomed us into his sister's home and ushered us toward the living room sofa.

"It was good of you to come," he said. "My wife, Lupe, will be out in a minute."

She arrived as promised, bearing a tray of cookies and lemonade in her graceful, tanned arms. We introduced ourselves and sipped the lemonade.

"We are so sorry for your loss," I began. "I can't even imagine what it's been like for the family."

Lupe rubbed her husband's huge shoulder. "It is hard on us, but harder on the children, I think. How do you tell them their nana was killed? They can understand death, but not this. They are too young."

"The morning after," I said, "Your sister's entire team called a meeting to talk about her. They said she was like a second mother; the kind of person who liked to take care of other people."

"That's our Anna," Thomas said with a proud smile. "She couldn't stop mothering people. When I was a boy twice her age, she would nag me about tying my shoes so I wouldn't trip and 'bust my ugly face'." He smiled at the memory.

"She loved her job," Lupe said. "And she was so excited about her promotion."

I glanced at Davis and he gave a tiny shrug.

"She sent Callie and Juan to a private school this year. She was so proud of them in their little uniforms. The teachers in the public school here, they try, but the school is not so good. Many students drop out."

"Who will raise the children now?" Davis asked.

"We will," Thomas said.

Lupe nodded and glanced toward the window. Outside, two young children were sitting in the grass playing with plastic cars. The boy smashed two cars together with explosive hand motions while his sister watched.

"Our children are grown," Lupe explained, "and Beth is not so stable. Perhaps she will be ready to be their mother again someday. Until then, they stay with us."

Lupe said this last bit with a determination that dared anyone to defy her; I doubted anyone would.

"Does Beth know about her Mother's passing?" I asked.

"We called the last number we had for her. Her... friend told us Beth is in California looking for work. He told us he would pass on the message, if she called," Lupe said. Thomas set his mouth in a thin line but did not speak.

Davis slid the benefits information out of the envelope. "Mr. Vasquez, you are Anna's next of kin, so this is for you."

I watched as Davis explained each item in the packet; the couple exhaled together when he told them we'd see to the children's medical needs for another year.

"That is a relief. We cannot put them on our plan until we arrange custody, and this will take time."

"I understand Anna left our life insurance program and got her own insurance," I said.

"We don't know if Anna had insurance or not," Lupe said, "anything we find will be a blessing."

The door opened, and I heard the clatter of feet on tile as the children ran into the house. "Tia! Tia!" The girl sobbed. "Juan hit me!" Lupe excused herself and went into the kitchen to soothe her niece. I asked Thomas if he had spoken to Detective Patterson.

"Yes. She has called us every day since it happened." His shoulders drooped. His voice grew quiet. "But she says there is nothing."

"Nothing?" Davis said.

"They say Anna might have been involved with a criminal organization. The detective has a good heart, but she's wrong." His tone betrayed his disappointment.

"Your sister's friends tell me she would never sell drugs. That the pills and money must have been planted," I said.

Davis looked at me, startled. I hadn't told him about the evidence at the crime scene.

Lupe returned and sat down. "I know what they found. And I don't think they would lie, but I also know my sister-in-law. Her heart never healed after Beth became an addict. There's no way she would profit from the misery of people like her daughter."

"This may be a strange question, but was there any chance Beth was involved? I'm not saying she would hurt her mother on purpose. It's just that I heard that Beth was in the area last month, and that she might have stolen Anna's car." I braced for an angry reply, or to be told to mind my own business, but Thomas just shook his head.

"That was a false alarm," he said. "And as strange as it sounds, it was wishful thinking. Anna was hoping Beth had borrowed her car, she was coming back home. It turns out the car was stolen by a man from Tacoma. He was caught by the police, and the car was returned. As far as we know, Beth has been out of state for months. She has outstanding warrants in King and Snohomish county for possession."

"Can you think of any reason someone would want to harm Anna?" I asked.

Lupe shook her head.

"My sister only had friends, not enemies." Thomas said. "I can't explain what the police found."

"Tell her what the coroner said," Lupe said.

"I insisted they test for drugs. They said there were none in her system. I hoped this would open the eyes of the police, but they say many dealers do not take the drugs; only sell them."

Thomas covered his eyes with a large hand and bent forward. His wife whispered something in his ear, and he nodded.

"Do you think they'll keep investigating?" I asked.

Thomas shrugged, and his eyes were moist. "They say they will look for more evidence, but I heard the truth in Detective Patterson's voice. Case closed. Unless someone walks in and admits their guilt, we'll never get justice for my sister."

"That's such bullshit." The words escaped my mouth before I knew it, and I couldn't retrieve them. Davis looked appalled, and Lupe's mouth formed an O.

"I'm sorry," I said. "I meant to say—"

"Don't be sorry," Thomas said. "I feel the same way."

"I'll pray for you all," Davis said quietly.

"Thank you both." Thomas grasped my small hand in his large one. Lupe embraced Davis, and then me. We returned to the car.

"Thanks for coming with me," I said as we pulled back into the employee parking lot. "I'm uncomfortable around grieving people, I'm never sure what to say."

"I'm glad I went," Davis said. "And I think you did just fine."

"Thomas said Anna was very happy with her promotion," I mused aloud.

"Right. What that was about? She was a File Clerk Three at the top of the pay band. Unless there was another supervisor job, she's red-circled." Davis pulled up the parking brake and turned off the car.

"Did you process a raise for her?"

"No. But, perhaps Shelby gave her special projects?" He suggested. "I've seen managers refer to someone as a 'lead' even when it's not formally a job title." Davis slowed his steps to accommodate my small ones.

"Sure, but it wouldn't explain why she was sending her grandkids to private school. Imaginary promotions don't come with real raises."

"So where did she get the money?"

"No idea," I said. We exchanged a glance, but neither of us wanted to say what was obvious. If she was dealing drugs that might explain the money.

"Are you going to the funeral?"

"Angela wants me to." Lupe had invited us as well, but I assumed she was being polite.

"Lupe and Thomas want you there. You should attend; it would mean a lot to them."

"I'll think about it. Funerals creep me out."

"No one likes funerals, Kat. They aren't something you do for yourself; go, and we'll cover you."

He was right, of course. And with the medical records team attending, it was an opportunity to find out where Anna's extra money was coming from.

CHAPTER SIXTEEN

AFTER WORK, I WALKED TO clear my head. Before hitting the street, I changed into jeans and a sweater and pulled my hair back into a ponytail. It was raining, and I didn't want wet hair in my eyes.

I turned onto Broadway and passed three hipster clothing stores, an adult toy shop, and half a dozen restaurants. On the way to Dick's Drive In, there's a red and white coffee cart that serves some of the best espresso in the city.

I ordered a latte and took a seat at one of the small round tables, under a dripping oak tree. There's something about the damp Seattle air that helps me think. That and caffeine, my constant companion.

I felt my conversations with Derek, Sally, Thomas, and Lupe bouncing around in the back of my mind like ping pong balls, vivid but disorganized. To clear my mind, I lifted the paper coffee cup to my nose and inhaled. The scent of caramel and vanilla filled my nostrils.

It wasn't until I was nearly back at the condo, my coffee cup empty and my sneakers soaked with rainwater, that I'd pinpointed the source of my restlessness.

I didn't want to believe Anna was a criminal, but it was starting to sound like truth. The lies about getting a promotion, the pills in her glove box, and the wad of cash in her car; what else could it be?

My job taught me there are few saints in this world, and even fewer villains. Most of us are a mix of good and bad, of triumphs and mistakes, muddling our way through life the best we can.

Perhaps Anna told herself she was just trying to support her grandchildren, and she convinced herself no one would get hurt. She wouldn't be the first person to go against her own values for monetary gain.

But if Anna led a double life, she'd fooled everyone, even those closest to her. Given her friendships with the women on her team, it was difficult to believe that no one would have noticed criminal activity, especially if it was right under their noses.

Besides, even if she was selling drugs, it didn't explain a fake robbery. Nothing about this situation made sense, and I wasn't going to believe she was a criminal simply because it was the easiest and most convenient explanation.

The evidence might be mixed, but I was sick of people making assumptions. Even my mother had remarked *'that Mexican woman who was selling drugs'* as if it were a settled matter and her death was a natural consequence of her behavior.

My heart protested that idea. Even if Anna had committed a crime, she didn't deserve to die.

Back at home, I turned off the lights in the living room and turned on some classical music. Outside my living room window, the city skyline was starting to sparkle.

I pulled out a legal pad and wrote down all the unanswered questions I could think of. First, the big question, and then the small ones.

1. Who killed Anna and why?
2. Why did Anna tell her family she got a promotion?
3. Was Anna dealing drugs? If not, where did she get private school tuition for her grandkids?
4. If she had brought drugs to work, who were her buyers? Were other employees involved?
5. If she wasn't dealing drugs, why would someone plant them on her?
6. Was Beth in town the night of October 31st?
7. Why did someone pretend to break into the pharmacy storeroom?

I thought hard and added one more item.

8. Did anyone in Medical Records have a criminal history?

If Anna was selling drugs, there had to be buyers. And someone with a drug conviction could be a potential link. Perhaps our background checks had missed something. I could check that out.

Also, I needed to find out if any of Anna's coworkers knew where her extra money was coming from.

With my list complete, I put on my pajamas and waited for Milo to climb into my lap. We watched television until bedtime, and I made a mental note of everyone I wanted to talk to after the funeral.

DRIVING TO CHURCH THE NEXT day, I tried to set my nervousness to one side. I'd never attended a formal memorial service before, and I wasn't sure what to expect. The pomp and ritual were unfamiliar, and I didn't know what the rules were.

After pausing at the large wooden doors outside the church, I saw Bridget, Sally, and two other clerks from Shelby's team approaching the stairs from the other side of the street. With a sigh of relief, I waited for them to catch up.

"You okay?" Bridget whispered after taking my arm and leading me up the stairs behind the rest of the women.

"I'm not much of a church goer," I confided. "I'm not sure what to do."

She patted my forearm. "It's fine. Just follow my lead."

Thomas was standing just inside the double doors with two men in their early sixties.

"Thank you so much for coming." Thomas shook my hand and embraced Bridget. "These are my brothers: Carlos and Tony."

"We worked with your sister," Bridget said. "We are so sorry for your loss, and we miss her."

They thanked us for coming, and then we walked up the center aisle, past a pedestal containing a large shallow dish of water. Bridget directed me down a row of wooden pews so heavily polished that they gleamed like glass. I sat and looked around.

There was a large altar in front of the church, a speaking pedestal off to one side, and an ornately carved display behind the altar, adorned with angels and hundreds of flowers.

Before long, the priest began walking back and forth across the front of the church, shaking what looked like a fancy maraca. Water flung outward from small holes in it, as he blessed the area.

"We are here today to celebrate the life of Anna Maria Vasquez, who has gone home to the kingdom." His tone was cheerful, as if he was sharing good news. He led the group in prayer, in the singing of hymns, and then asked who would like to speak.

Thomas went to the podium and told a story about how Anna used to protect him from bullies at school, even when she was half his size. This brought a wave of smiles through the tears. Lupe read a bible passage and talked about how Anna had welcomed her as a sister. She shared how Anna comforted her through several miscarriages and the death of her own father.

The priest was walking up to the podium when I heard a sudden intake of breath from the other side of the pews.

A painfully thin woman with long dark hair obscuring most of her features was walking up the center of the aisle. The priest walked forward to help her up to the podium and then stood to one side as she spoke. When she pushed her hair out of her face, I saw a sickly young woman facing us. Her skin had a yellowish cast, and she had the look of a wraith.

"My mother was always there for me," she began, her voice quavering and almost childlike. "I have not always made the best choices in my life, and yet she always told me she loved me. When I couldn't be well, she loved my children as if they were her own and provided them with a good life."

In the front pew, I saw Lupe and Thomas put their arms around Juan and Callie.

"Jesus taught us that he who is without sin should cast the first stone," Beth said, looking down. "My mother lived by those words. She never judged. She always chose love. If you can hear me mama, I want to say thank you, and I love you too."

She stood in place for a moment until the priest leaned to whisper in her ear. He led her to the family pew where her aunts and uncles embraced her in turn.

The priest asked everyone to stand and sing Anna's favorite hymn.

"Amazing Grace, how sweet the sound. That saved a wretch like me. All was lost but now I'm found. I was blind, but now I see."

Bridget handed me a tissue. I wiped my eyes and followed the procession down the aisle and out to the street.

CHAPTER SEVENTEEN

AFTER THE FUNERAL, THE MOURNERS scattered, heading back to their cars. Most of the medical records team had attended, along with a smattering of other hospital staff. If I wanted to talk to people about Anna, I'd need to do it at work.

Beth's arrival had surprised and touched me. She was clearly sick, and Lupe ushered her into a car as soon as the service ended. Her comments made it unlikely she'd been involved in her mother's death, but I'd try to speak with her when she was stronger.

Back at the office I stopped in the mailroom to check my inbox. Akiko was nearby making copies.

"How was the funeral?" she asked.

"Intense," I said. "Sad but uplifting at the same time."

"Makes sense. Catholics believe when you die, assuming you were a good person, you go to heaven. We miss the dead, but we expect to join them again someday."

The copy machine ceased its rhythmic clatter. She picked up a stack of stapled packets and tapped them into a uniform pile.

"Did I miss anything important while I was gone?" I asked.

"Nope. I'm teaching an interview class to our front desk supervisors today; then I've got a grievance meeting in pediatrics. No emergencies."

"Okay. Call me if you need anything. I need to catch up on morning emails and prep for our benefits renewal presentation."

Akiko made a face. "Good luck with that one. How is it looking so far?"

"Davis says fifteen percent increases, if we're lucky."

"Oh, joy," she said.

I left her to her work and went to my office to deal with the pile of tasks that awaited me.

AFTER LUNCH, I WANTED TO find Shelby Cooper. I had questions, and she might hold some answers.

"Are you heading out?" Jocelyn asked as I walked by her desk.

"Yes, but not for long. Call my cell if you need anything." After a moment's hesitation, I added the following, "I'd like us to do an audit of our criminal background checks for all the departments located on the lower level. medical records, IT, compliance, and pharmacy. If anyone has a background check over two years old, let's rerun it."

"Did the police ask you to do that?" Jocelyn asked.

"Nope, just taking initiative."

"Got it," she said, fist-bumping me before I resumed walking.

Inside medical records, Shelby was stacking boxes of patient charts on a heavy-duty cart. I waited while the courier handed Shelby a clipboard. She reviewed the page closely and signed it. He smiled as she handed the clipboard back to him, then leaned forward to whisper something to her. She blushed and accepted the carbon copy of the form he handed her.

"Thank you, James. Tomorrow same time," Shelby said. She turned to see me standing near her office door and jerked backward in surprise. "Oh! Hi Kat."

I stepped back to make room for the cart. The guy was cute in a geeky sort of way, with softly curling red hair tucked under a baseball cap. He winked at me as he passed.

"Your whole team was at the service," I said to Shelby. "How did you accomplish that feat?"

She smiled. "Two MAs from the ER came in on their day off to cover."

"That was nice of them. Do you have a minute? Something odd came up."

"Sure." She leaned against the wall outside her office.

"Anna told a few people she had gotten a promotion. Do you know anything about that?"

Shelby looked puzzled. "A promotion? A promotion to what?"

"I have no idea."

Shelby frowned. "Me either. We don't have the budget for a lead position, so she was already in the top job available, she was a level three."

"That's what I thought. Is it possible she was exaggerating a little? Did you ever refer to her as the lead, even informally? That happens, sometimes."

"No, I'm careful about stuff like that. Besides, on my days off, I have Amy cover for me. She's got her health information management degree, so she's the most qualified." She crossed her arms. "That was a weird thing for Anna to say."

I shrugged. "It probably doesn't matter. One more thing. Did you notice anything strange in the department over the last few weeks, either before or after Anna died?"

"Strange like what?"

"I'm not sure. But I'm wondering if there is anything that might shed light on what happened. I'm not talking about anything suspicious, just any out of the ordinary occurrences. Like having more visitors to the department or any unexpected problems. Surprises, basically. Any events that left you feeling puzzled."

Shelby seemed confused, and I realized I wasn't explaining myself very well. "The police told Thomas and Lupe that they are winding down the investigation," I said. "But I want to make sure we do everything we can to help. No stone unturned."

She frowned and then shook her head.

"No, nothing I can think of. Sorry."

A voice piped up from behind one of the file racks.

"What about the misfiles?"

I had forgotten that speaking in medical records is like having a conversation in public. You never know who's listening on the other side of the file rack.

"What misfiles?" I asked.

Amy walked around the corner and set a stack of files down on an empty cart. She grasped one hand in the other and stretched her hand back and forth at the wrist. I recognized the stretch as one our employee health nurse taught to prevent repetitive stress injuries.

"It was the day after Anna died. We were doing our work like usual when I saw there was a file in the wrong place. Not one digit off—that happens—but way wrong, like it was crammed in the stacks at random. I pulled it, but then Bridget found one, too. We walked the whole department and found twenty misfiled charts in total."

"That's weird," I said.

"It was," Shelby said, nodding. "I figured the police must have found the files on the ground and stuck them back. Careless of them, but I suppose they had other things on their minds."

"Could Anna have done it?" I asked.

"No way! She was super accurate," Amy said. "Besides, it was so obvious. A clerk two days on the job wouldn't file so badly."

"Thanks, Amy. I don't know what it means, but it's worth noting."

"Anytime." She grabbed her stack of files and disappeared in the stacks again. I looked at Shelby and inclined my head toward her office. She took the hint, followed me inside, and shut the door.

"What do you think?" I asked.

She shrugged. "Who knows? Mistakes aren't unheard of. One of the clerks might have done it if they were in a hurry to leave. They can't go home until their cart is empty."

"Do you have a list of those files? The ones that were put back wrong?"

She shook her head. "We refiled them."

I took a breath and asked the question that made me uneasy. "Could Anna have been selling drugs like the police said? You've worked with her for a long time, you knew her better than most."

"If you asked me a week ago, I'd say no. But I heard what the police found, and it sounds like she lied about getting a promotion, right?"

"It does," I said.

"Well, I don't want to believe she'd do such a thing," Shelby said, "but it's getting harder not to. Perhaps I didn't know her as well as I thought? I'm still hoping there's an innocent explanation, for the family's sake."

"Me too," I said. But if there was such an explanation, it wasn't lying around in the file room waiting to be picked up.

CHAPTER EIGHTEEN

I SPENT THE REMAINDER OF the afternoon shaping benefits projections into a presentation for the executive team. Sadly, no amount of cheerful clip-art could hide that healthcare costs for a medical assistant could cost more than his or her annual salary.

I sent my first draft to Davis so he could double check my work and add in the supporting documentation. My computer chimed, and I pulled up my email.

> To: Katherine Voyzey
> From: Sally Jacobs
> Subject: Coffee
>
> Hey, can you meet me and Bridget at the downstairs Starbucks at five? We want an update.

I replied to say I'd be there. Sally knew how to use a subject line to get my attention.

When I arrived, the women were seated around a square wooden table near the front window. They waved at me through the glass as I approached. I ordered myself a grande mocha with extra whipped cream and took the seat opposite the window.

"We want to talk to you about a few things," Sally said.

"Sure." I pulled off the lid to my coffee so I could access the whipped cream directly. *Glorious.*

"First, did you tell the police about the pharmacy door?" Bridget asked.

"I did. They didn't ask any follow-up questions; To be honest, I'm not sure they thought it was a big deal."

"After all we did!" Sally said. "We had to twist Matt's arm pretty hard to get him to talk to you."

"I noticed. How did you find out, anyway?"

"He looked guilty, so I pinned him down. The man wears his heart on his sleeve." Sally looked pleased with herself.

"We hear you're doing some investigating of your own," Bridget said, raising an eyebrow.

"Amy told us about your conversation with Shelby." Sally said. "She wanted to be here, but she had to go to her other job."

"She has a second job?" I was surprised; our file clerks all work full time.

Bridget nodded. "About half of us do. It's a great job when you're on your own, but with a family sixteen dollars an hour doesn't go far in this town." She glanced at her watch. "I don't mean to rush this, but I need to catch my bus in twenty minutes. Have you learned anything new?"

"Do either of you hear about Anna getting a promotion?" I asked.

I told them what Thomas said about the promotion and how Anna was sending her grandkids to a private elementary school.

"She didn't get a promotion," Sally said.

"I know. I asked Shelby, and she confirmed it. There are no positions in the department for her to be promoted into."

"We're fully aware," Bridget said. "It stinks."

Sally was thinking. "You know, she mentioned the school fees once. She said she got some money from a scholarship."

"If she got a scholarship, why would she tell her sister she got a promotion?" Bridget asked.

"It sounds like she was trying to hide the source of the money." My disappointment must have shone through because Sally patted my hand.

"Don't worry. I'm sure there's a reasonable explanation. We'll ask around for you."

"Thanks," I said. "Also, I'm curious about something. Amy told me there were a bunch of files put in the wrong place the morning after the murder."

"That's true," Bridget said. "We thought maybe the police stuck them in there when they were cleaning up."

"That's what I heard. But I doubt the police would have messed with the filed. Could Anna have put them back that way?"

"I doubt it," Sally said. She drained the last bit of coffee from her cup. "Anna was meticulous. She'd never just shove records in the stacks like that. Besides, it would be stupid. We'd catch it in, like, two seconds."

"Could you find those misfiled charts again?" I asked.

"Normally, no." Bridget said. "When we see a misfile we just stick it back where it belongs."

"Normally?"

"Well, I figured if the police crammed them back in the stacks, they might also have been careless enough to lose a few of the pages.

"That's why I added them to my audit. We pull a random set of files every week and check them for completeness and make sure everything is where it should be. You'd be amazed how often someone's test result ends up in the wrong chart, for example."

"So, you checked them," I said. "Do you remember if they had anything in common?"

Bridget frowned, thinking hard. "No. I did a quick audit to make sure the pages were ordered correctly, and they had the correct names on them. I don't read the files; a person's medical issues are none of my business."

"But you still have a list of those charts?"

"Yeah, there's a logbook. That way if we have a doctor consistently messing things up, we can talk to them. Why?"

Shelby hadn't offered that information. Then again, she might not have known Bridget checked those files.

"Could you pull them again?" I asked.

"I suppose," Bridget said slowly, "but accessing patient information for non-official reasons is a fireable offense. And I try to avoid those."

"But you don't want any patient info, right?" Sally said to me. "You want to see if those files have anything in common."

"Exactly. But not if it'll get you fired. I'm grasping at straws here; there might not be anything to find. And my hunch isn't worth your job."

"Oh, don't worry about it," Sally made a flicking motion with one hand. "I'll re-audit those files this week. I won't share any patient information, but it can't hurt to make sure they were all refiled in the right place. Bridget can get sloppy with her work sometimes." She winked at her coworker, who didn't look at all pleased with this idea.

"Did you find out if Beth was in town the night of the murder?" Bridget asked.

I shook my head. "Thomas and Lupe are pretty sure she was out-of-state. Nothing concrete though."

Bridget pulled out her cell phone and looked at the time.

"I need to run. Anything else?"

"Maybe."

"Spit it out. I've got places to be."

"Is it just me, or is Shelby acting weird? When I showed up today she almost jumped, like she was surprised to see me. And her face was red."

"Oh. That!" Bridget said, her mouth quirking upward.

"Yes, that," Sally replied. She grinned at her coworker. "We pretend not to notice, but everyone knows."

"She's dating James, the delivery guy," Bridget added.

"He passes her love notes," Sally said with a conspiratorial smile. "It's adorable, but it's technically against the what-do-you-call-it?"

"Fraternization policy?"

"Yeah, that one."

"A secret romance." Sally sighed dramatically, fluttering her eyelashes. "If only I could be so lucky."

"You won't get her in trouble?" Bridget asked. "It's a stupid rule, and it's good to see her so happy."

I bit back a retort. Someday, somewhere, an HR person would have a conversation without being accused of tattling to corporate. "I have bigger fish to fry," I said.

"Okay. Bridge and I will see what we can find out about Anna's scholarship fake-promotion thingy, and I'll double check those patient charts for—"

"Sally, I don't know—" Bridget warned.

"Accuracy."

"Thanks, ladies," I said. "We'll keep looking for answers until we run out of leads."

We said our goodbyes, and the two women plunged into the rain. After I finished my coffee, I followed suit.

CHAPTER NINETEEN

THERE'S A LOT OF CRYING in my line of work. It's awkward, but when someone gets passed over for promotion, or when they're being fired, waterworks can happen.

You get used to it. We're all human, after all. But it's different when it's one of your own people doing the weeping. Normally Akiko is the one keeping a cool head while I'm ready to leap out a window. So when I saw her sitting at her desk with her face in her hands, I felt a jolt of alarm.

"Akiko," I spoke quietly to avoid startling her, "what's wrong?"

She looked up, and I saw her black eyeliner had run down her face, and her nose was cherry red. She wiped her eyes, smearing the mess around. She sat up and took a sharp breath.

"I'm okay. I just need a minute to shake this off."

"I'll be right back," I said. I stepped across the hall to our bathroom and ran warm water over a few paper towels, returned to her office, and handed them to her.

"You've got raccoon eyes."

She wiped her face. I took a seat opposite her and shut the door behind me. As the foundation and eye makeup came off, I noticed how young she looked. Fourteen instead of twenty-nine.

"Angela hates me," Akiko said.

"Angela is upset with people on a daily basis," I replied, feeling weary. "What did she say?"

"Remember Jackie, the new ultrasound tech?"

I nodded.

"Well, she dozed off at orientation during Gary's presentation."

I winced. Gary Westerman is our CEO, and he always comes to meet the new staff. He's an enthusiastic speaker, but he loves to pontificate. There was a time or two I needed to pinch myself to stay awake, too.

"That's awkward," I said.

"I know, right?" she said. "It was late in the day, and Erin cranked up the heat because it was so cold out. You know how everyone gets tired after lunch.

"Well, Jackie dozed off and Angela heard about it, then she called me into her office," Akiko's eyes watered again, and she grabbed a tissue from the box on her desk. "She said it was an embarrassment to the company to hire people with such poor judgment, and that she wanted me to make sure this never happened again."

I sighed. "I'm sorry."

"How much trouble am I in?"

"Zero," I said.

"That's not what it sounded like," she said. "Angela didn't want you to hire me. She thinks I'm a loser. And now she thinks I'm a horrible recruiter too."

"Look," I said, "Angela is a smart woman. She does a lot of good for this company, but it doesn't stop her from charging over people like a human bulldozer. It's her weakness, and it has nothing to do with you."

Akiko seemed unconvinced.

"Listen. Three weeks ago, Angela called me and told me I was losing control of the department because there were crumbs on the table in the reception area."

This earned me a small smile. "Really?"

"Yup. She said if I couldn't keep our lobby clean, I needed to find a new receptionist."

Akiko's eyes widened, but I just shrugged.

"Did I go running to Jocelyn to tell her that her days are numbered? No. I wiped down the table myself and asked Jocelyn to keep a close eye on it for the next few months. After a while, Angela will find another target."

"So, you ignore her?" Akiko sat up straighter in her chair.

"Not at all. I try to listen to what she's communicating without taking her style personally. It's bad that Jackie fell asleep in orientation. I agree with that and so do you. We should call Michelle and tell her what happened so she can keep a close eye on Jackie during the probationary period."

"I did that today," Akiko said.

"Good. You handled it perfectly. Where I don't agree with Angela is that it's somehow HR's fault when an occasional employee goes off the rails. If you were recruiting people left and right who couldn't remain conscious, then I'd be worried. Either that, or we'd have to start spiking the water fountains with caffeine."

Akiko smiled. "Thanks for making me feel better, and I'm sorry I lost it."

"You didn't lose anything. We all need a good cry now and again. Besides, you'll return the favor the next time I'm convinced I'm the most terrible manager on earth, right?"

"Right." She looked at the black makeup smeared on the paper towels. "Ugh. I need to go reapply my face."

People like Angela are why we put our armor on when we go to work, I thought. That armor might be professionalism, or a nice business suit, or even some thick black mascara. We want a barrier between the 'real us' and the person we need to be at work. Usually that's enough to get us through the day, but sometimes it isn't.

I left Akiko in her office and walked back to mine, letting my pleasant expression relax into a more accurate scowl.

Angela and I had a tense relationship at times, but the upside was that she doesn't interfere with my people. Her attack on my generalist crossed an invisible line, and I was pissed.

It was less than an hour until I was due to give my benefits presentation to the executive team, and I needed to wrestle my emotions back under control. I took a few deep breaths and played upbeat music on my computer. It wasn't good enough, but it would have to do.

ACCORDING TO *HR MAGAZINE*, PUBLIC speaking is the most common phobia in the world. Fortunately, when they were handing out phobias, I didn't get that one. On the flip side, I received a wicked addiction to people-pleasing, and my left breast is slightly larger than the right one. I'm not sure this was a fair trade.

As soon as the executive team was gathered around their shiny conference room table (so much nicer than ours!), I pulled up my first slide and cut right to the chase. "Today, I'll be giving you an overview of our expected premium increases for employee benefits for the upcoming year and sharing three options for cost control."

It took only ten minutes to share the news, none of which was good. If we kept our same benefits plan the following year, it would cost us an additional 1.5 million dollars.

Susan, our VP of Marketing, raised her hand to get our attention, "You showed us pricing from the same three vendors we looked at last year. What were the rates from the other three brokers?"

"Sorry, I'm not sure which brokers you mean."

She turned to my boss. "Remember? Those companies I sent you last month? From the conference in San Diego. They said they could beat our current rates." Susan looked to me. "Didn't you get them?"

Angela waved her hand impatiently. "Yes, I did send them over last month to Katherine, but they probably got lost in the shuffle. You know how much email she gets." Her tone was dismissive. "Kat, go find the message from me and follow up on getting bids from those three. We'll have you come back here when you've completed your work." She fixed me with an intense stare for half a beat and then inspected her manicure.

I stood there stupidly for a moment, processing what had just gone down. Had she thrown me under the bus in front of everyone? I gave her a curt nod. "I'll get right on that."

"Let's table this conversation for today," Angela glanced at the meeting agenda and gestured toward our CFO. "Gary, if you agree, let's move to financials. Katherine, you have things to do. You can go."

Our CFO shot me a pitying look and passed out financial statements. I beat a hasty retreat toward the door.

When I got back to my office, I took a deep breath and forced myself to triple check my email. I reviewed my spam folder. I searched my archives. Nothing.

Angela blamed me for something she forgot to do. And worst of all, she'd made me look incompetent in front of the entire executive team.

I strode out of my office and blurted, "I'm going for a walk." It must have come out louder than I expected because Jocelyn looked startled. I gave her what I hoped was a reassuring smile and told her I'd be back in half an hour.

I walked around the hospital ten times, stomping my feet against the pavement and kicking up mounds of autumn leaves as I went.

RAGE-WALKING AROUND THE BUILDING WAS cathartic, but I needed to get my act together. "Don't jump to conclusions" was one of my mottos and I needed to walk the talk. After all, it was possible Angela hadn't thrown me under the bus, but that she simply made a mistake. Maybe she thought she'd sent the email, but she forgot. And aren't we all fallible?

When I opened my email again, I saw Angela had just forwarded me the message that Susan sent her a few months ago. I'd set messages from Angela to be flagged in red, and it glowed in my inbox like a cinder.

I printed it out and walked it to Davis.

"How did the benefits presentation go?" he asked.

"It went okay. Unfortunately, I got a request to get bids from three more brokers."

He stared at the print-out for a moment. I was asking him to redo a month's worth of work. Not to mention, our current broker would be pissed if she knew we were considering an out-of-state stranger.

"If I had anticipated this, we could have done it with the others. I'm sorry for the hassle," I said.

Davis sighed, "We do what we gotta do."

I left him to his task, feeling guilty about wasting his time. Angela didn't do it on purpose, I reminded myself. She probably just forgot.

HAVING TALKED MYSELF OUT OF being pissed off, I was feeling better. That is, until I met with our CFO that afternoon.

"Come on in," April said, gathering stacks of paper off her guest table to make room. Her office was always a disaster. The walls were covered in sticky notes and computer printouts, and her whiteboard was a mess of numbers and lines connecting them.

"Someday you're going to make an archaeologist very happy," I quipped, pointing at her wall of colorful stickies.

"Huh?"

"Those are hieroglyphs, right?"

She smiled "My husband says I have the handwriting of a physician."

April needed help coaching one of her supervisors who had a habit of talking down to his employees. After we worked that out, she asked if she could return the favor.

"What do you mean?" I asked.

"You gave me good advice, and I'm wondering if I can give you some too," she spoke hesitantly, and I could tell she was worried about offending me.

"Sure," I said.

"I wish you wouldn't let Angela walk all over you like that. It's painful to watch, and it reflects poorly upon you."

"You mean what happened today at the meeting?"

"One example of many."

I shrugged. April meant well, but she reported directly to the CEO. No one was going to fire her for speaking her mind.

"I hear you, but I don't know what I could have done. She's my boss. It's not like I can call her a liar. Besides, she probably thought she sent me that email. It wasn't intentional."

"You're not stupid, Kat. There's no reason for you to be a doormat." She looked at me over her wire frame glasses. "We need a strong HR director here, desperately. Someone who won't cave when a powerful person tells them no.

"It's your job to speak up for what is right and wrong. How can we trust you to do that, if you won't even stand up for yourself?"

"That's a little harsh, isn't it? I know how to stand up for myself." My face felt hot, and the knowledge that I was blushing made me even more embarrassed.

"Perhaps," she said, her tone softening. "I know you mean well, and I'm not in a position to tell you to do anything. You can dismiss my advice, but I hope you'll think it over."

"I will," I said.

She looked at me with doubt in her eyes, I probably should have been more appreciative of her attempt to help me, but I didn't feel grateful. Her words were one more punch in the gut, and I was tired of taking punches.

By the time I dragged myself across the threshold of my condo that evening, I felt numb. Inside my bedroom, I shed my work clothes into a puddle around my feet, got directly into my

Hello Kitty pajamas, and went into the kitchen to make dinner. As I watched my pathetic tray of pasta spin in the microwave, I wondered if April was right.

Was I too weak to stand up when someone was doing something wrong? I didn't like that notion, but I couldn't bring up any evidence to refute it.

CHAPTER TWENTY

SLEEP MUST WORK MIRACLES BECAUSE I arrived at the office feeling renewed. Be it hiring, firing, or slapping new hires awake at orientation, I was ready for anything. And it was good timing because mid-morning I got an email from Sally.

> To: Katherine Voyzey
> From: Sally Jacobs
> Subject: Lunch Meeting
>
> The Medical Records Crime Fighters Club requests the pleasure of your company for lunch.
>
> PS: You won't believe what we found.

I responded that I'd be there. My phone rang. It was Akiko.
"Question," she said.
"Fire away."
"I'm screening candidates for the file clerk position, and someone asked me why the job is open. And I totally choked."
"What did you say?"

"I said she left for personal reasons. Seriously, personal reasons? What was I thinking?"

"Well, you didn't lie, and you didn't offer to show them crime scene photos. It could have been far worse."

"Very funny. What's our official answer?"

I thought for a moment. "Keep it simple and say we're hiring because the employee died recently. Anyone we hire will learn about the circumstances, but we don't need to bring it up." Anna's termination would be coded in our system as involuntary turnover, reason: deceased.

"Works for me. It's better than sticking my foot in my mouth."

"True. Foot-in-mouth removal isn't cheap."

"Is it more expensive than head-in-ass removal?"

"I'm not sure our plan covers that," I said. "Otherwise I'd be making referrals left and right."

"Me too. I'll make you a list of people who need that procedure," she said, laughing. I hung up the phone with a new lightness in my heart. Akiko was joking around again. And Sally had found something out. Something useful? I hoped so. My day was looking up.

LATER, I LOOKED FOR SALLY and Bridget; they were sitting at a table in the corner of the cafeteria, half-hidden behind potted plants. After procuring a grilled cheese sandwich and a cup of tomato soup, I joined them.

"Is this the Holy Heart Crime Fighting Club?"

Sally grinned. "You liked that, huh?"

"I'm honored to be part of such an elite group. What's the news?"

Sally said, "Bridge, why don't you go first?"

The older woman put down her sandwich. "You said Anna claimed she got a promotion," she said.

I nodded. "Did she talk to someone about it?"

"Kinda. She told Martha that she had taken on a side job to make extra money for the grandkids."

"Did she tell her what it was?" I asked.

"Unfortunately, no. Martha got the impression she was excited about it, but it was kind of a secret."

That was a disappointment. I hoped at least one of Anna's coworkers would know the truth. A promotion, a scholarship, and now a side job? It seemed Anna told a different story depending upon the audience.

"She told Martha the commissions were good, and that she got money for each person she referred. That sounds like a sales job, right? Commissions?"

"Could be," I said. "And don't take my head off for saying it, but a drug dealer might use that language."

"I don't know," Sally said. "It sounds more like she was getting kickbacks. Besides, if she was dealing drugs, which she wasn't, she wouldn't tell Martha about it at all."

"Well done," I said. "I don't understand what it means yet, but it's more than we had yesterday. Did you learn anything else?"

"Not about the side job," Sally said. "But I found something odd about those misfiles." She paused for effect and took a slow bite of her sandwich.

"Well, don't leave me hanging," I said.

"The misfiled charts belonged to dead patients."

"What?"

"They all died within the last year. It gets weirder though."

"Weirder than that?"

Bridget picked up the thread. "When a patient dies, we pull the chart and send it to be archived. If a patient's family member requests an archived file, we fill out a request and get the file back."

Sally jumped in. "Most of the misfiles were returned to us from storage. I called the vendor, and they said Anna filled out the request forms. It didn't raise any red flags because they assumed she was doing so on behalf of a family member."

"But she wasn't?" I asked.

"Not that I can tell." Sally said.

"But what does it mean? Why would Anna request a bunch of files for dead patients?"

"I have no idea," Bridget said. "Sally got it into her head that this is some sort of mass-murder scheme and that all the patients were poisoned." She shook her head a little.

Sally shrugged. "I read a lot of Agatha Christie. She wrote about untraceable poisons."

I leaned forward and whispered, "Does it look like they were murdered?"

Sally grinned. "You're as bad as I am. No, I took a quick peek, and it was natural causes stuff. Cancer, heart attack, aneurysm, even one from pneumonia."

"Did they all have the same doctor?" I asked.

"Nope, different docs, different medical problems. Most of them were old and sick. Nothing else to tie them together."

"Except that they're dead."

"Right," Sally said.

We all looked at each other.

"Yeah, we're stumped too," Sally said.

"Can I get a list of their names?" Then I quickly added, "Don't show me the files or any medical information. Just the names. I'll look them up on the internet and see if I can discover a connection between them."

"Sure. I'll drop the list by your office later," Sally said. "But to be clear, we are officially breaking the rules now. If Shelby finds out, she'll have my head."

"Do you want to stop?" I wouldn't blame them if they did, but I had a feeling they were as curious as I was.

Sally shook her head.

"No, we're in," Bridget said. "We want to see this through."

I nodded. "This feels like the first useful bit of information we've found. And I'll ask Thomas and Lupe about this side job of Anna's. Maybe there was paperwork in her house?"

Bridget looked at the clock and nudged Sally with one arm. "That sounds like a plan, keep us posted, okay?"

"I will." They left me alone at the table, and I finished my sandwich. It occurred to me that I wasn't bending the rules so much as I was breaking them. Sally sharing patient information with me could get all of us fired.

Me! Aiding and abetting the violation of a corporate policy. The bigger injustice would be letting the murderer get away, but still I felt uneasy. I'd stepped off the responsible path, and onto another one. The territory was unfamiliar, but I had to keep going.

DURING MY ONE-ON-ONE WITH ANGELA that afternoon, I could hear April's lecture ringing in my ears.

"You're certain the family isn't going to sue us," Angela was asking, her face twisted with skepticism. "I'm having a difficult time believing that. Perhaps I should have our attorney call them and—"

"We don't need to be so heavy-handed. They were happy I spoke to them, and they seemed touched that we offered a year of medical coverage for the grandkids. I can't read their minds or predict the future, but I doubt we'll have a problem."

"We should have had them sign a release of claims, holding us harmless. We could require they sign it in exchange for the extra insurance."

"I don't know," I said, shaking my head. "We left things on a positive note, and documents from lawyers might ruin that."

Angela sighed and clicked the button on the back of her retractable pen. "Fine. I agree we shouldn't spook them. But next time something like this happens, I'm sending one of our attorneys no matter what Gary says."

I took a breath and summoned my courage for what I was about to say next. My rehearsal in the shower that morning had sounded pretty good, but the rubber duck I'd been talking to wasn't half so intimidating.

"I talked to Davis about those benefits bids you asked for. He said the new broker isn't very educated about the Washington State market. It'll take two weeks to get a bid, but they say it will be ten percent higher than our current offer, at least. Do you want us to keep researching?"

"No, I just needed to keep Susan happy. She gets offended if we don't jump on every little referral she sends us even if they're random people she met at a conference."

I cleared my throat and tried to ignore the pounding in my chest. "Um. You said you'd sent me Susan's email a while back, but I didn't have it until yesterday."

"Ah. That's fine." Angela had half-turned to her computer screen.

"It's just that I felt embarrassed in front of the execs," I said. "When it looked like I hadn't done my job."

Angela shot me an amused look. "You're saying I blamed you for my screw-up."

"Well, I don't want to assume—"

"You're right; I did use you."

Before I could formulate a response, Angela was waving her hand dismissively. "Susan was playing one of her little games, trying to make me look bad in front of Gary. Everyone knew it. I wanted you to cover for me, and you did. That's what teammates do, right?"

"Ah," I stammered. "I guess so."

"Is there anything else?"

"No. I'm glad we cleared that up."

"Good."

"Also, I'm re-running criminal background checks for everyone who works downstairs. If there was a drug-related crime on campus, I want to make sure nothing else slipped through the cracks."

An honest-to-God smile flashed across Angela's face. "That's good. Let's put this mess behind us as soon as possible."

When I got back to my office, Jocelyn handed me an interoffice envelope. I unwound the string and opened the flap, inside was a neatly printed list of names, courtesy of Sally Jacobs.

Now that I had the names of the dead patients, all I needed was a web browser.

CHAPTER TWENTY-ONE

WHEN I GOT HOME, I made myself dinner. Well, I ordered delivery from Broadway Thai, but I put the food on a real plate and used a cloth napkin. That's as close to cooking as I like to get.

The condo's security guard doesn't even call me when the food delivery people arrive these days. He sees someone carrying a paper bag the approximate size and shape of a takeout order and sends them to my floor.

As I ate, I reviewed the materials I'd set out on my coffee table. Milo walked back and forth across the pages and meowed. I offered him some of my curry but he turned up his nose at it and ran to the front door.

"Derek isn't coming. It's just us tonight."

Milo gave me a look of disgust and groomed his tail. I reviewed my original list of questions about the murder

1. Who killed Anna and why?
2. Why did Anna tell her family she got a promotion?
3. Was Anna dealing drugs? If not, where did she get private school tuition for her grandkids?

4. If she had brought drugs to work, who were her buyers? Was another staff member involved?
5. If she was not dealing drugs why would someone plant them on her?
6. Was Beth in town the night of October 31st?
7. Why did someone pretend to break into the pharmacy storeroom?
8. Did anyone in medical records have a criminal history?

I hadn't made much progress, but I could add a few questions to the list.

9. Why were charts misfiled the morning after the murder?
10. Other than being dead, what did those patients have in common?
11. Why had Anna requested those files be returned to Holy Heart?

I picked up the phone and dialed Detective Patterson's number. She answered on the first ring.

"Detective? This is Kat from Holy Heart. Do you have a minute?"

"Sure. Evans told me about your last call." Was it just me, or did I hear a hint of amusement in her voice? "Do you have something else for us?"

"Yes. Anna's daughter Beth is back in town. She showed up at the funeral, and I thought you might want to talk to her."

"Good to know, we'll check in with her. Anything else?"

"Maybe. The morning after the murder, the clerks found a bunch of files stuck in the wrong places in the file room."

"And that's unusual?"

"Yes. There was a cart tipped over during the attack. And I was wondering, was there any chance someone from the police took the files on the ground and stuck them back in the racks? I thought that might explain them being out of order."

"Nope. Our techs photographed the scene, and anything not deemed evidence is left alone. We didn't take any files with us; they would have been left on the ground or on a surface nearby. Who told you they were put in the wrong place?"

I looked at the list of names on my coffee table and decided not to go into any more detail than necessary. "One of the clerks mentioned it when I was down there. Her name is Amy."

"I appreciate you telling me." Patterson sounded thoughtful as she said, "What else?"

She knows I'm holding onto something, I thought.

"Rumor has it Anna was earning extra cash and sending her grandkids to a private school. She told her family she got a promotion, but there was no promotion. But she told another coworker that she had a side job, and another that she got a scholarship for the kids."

"I see," she said.

"This doesn't prove she was a drug dealer."

"Uh-huh." There was that amused tone again. "Anything else?"

"No, that's it for now. Any new leads on your end, or is it case-closed, like I've been hearing?"

"Well, I hear it's important for investigators to do their jobs and investigate—"

"Ah, I'm sorry about my outburst to your partner. I wasn't trying to be mean."

"Don't worry about it," she said. "And if you find anything else that piques your curiosity, give me a call. The case isn't closed if that's what you're worried about. Investigations take time, but we're nowhere close to giving up."

"Thanks," I said.

"Anytime. I gotta run, but I'll be in touch."

CHAPTER TWENTY-TWO

THE NEXT MORNING, SALLY POKED her head around the corner of my doorway. "Got a sec?"

"Sure, come in and shut the door." I stood up and stretched. "No news yet. I spent half the night trying to find a connection between those names you gave me, but no luck yet."

Elderly people don't have much of an internet footprint, I'd discovered. I found a handful of memorial Facebook pages, and while most of the deceased had obituaries, as far as I could tell all they had in common was our hospital.

"Something weird happened," Sally dropped into a chair across from me.

"Are you okay?" I asked. She looked shaken, and her fingernails were bitten to the quick.

"Yeah, just worried. I went home early yesterday; one of my kids had a thing. I sent you those names, and today when I came in, I figured I'd write them for myself too, so I could look them up on the internet. You know, two heads being better than one."

"Sure."

"I pulled the audit book, and the page was torn out."

"Maybe Bridget took it out, when she was gathering information."

"Nope. I asked her."

"Why would someone take the page out?"

"I don't know, but it's concerning, isn't it? What if the murderer knows we're snooping around, and they don't like it?"

"Who else worked with you yesterday?"

"Normally it's just me and Bridget on the swing shift. Amy came in to cover for me."

"Do you think Amy took it?"

"I don't see why."

"Perhaps she got the same idea we did, and she was checking the names?"

Sally's forehead furrowed. "That could be! She was the one who noticed the misfiles. Should I ask her?"

I wasn't sure. On the one hand, it would make us feel better if there was an innocent explanation. But on the other, if Bridget and Sally were being watched, asking more questions could put them in danger. "If someone's trying to stop us from investigating this murder—"

"We shouldn't draw attention to ourselves.".

"Exactly."

"But we might be getting close to something; I don't want to give up," she said, before biting a fingernail.

I thought about what Shelby told me about Sally. She had young kids at home, and they were counting on her. I wanted to keep Bridget and Sally far away from danger, but how could I demand they stop digging if I wasn't willing to do that myself?

Sally must have read my expression because she crossed her arms. "We're not backing out, and neither should you."

"I won't, but we need to be careful. Make sure you stick close to Bridget; keep an eye on each other."

"We will. Now are you going to give me the list of names or not?"

"Okay," I replied, "but no more meeting in the lunch room, and no more snooping around during office hours. And if anyone else knows you've been investigating, tell them it was all dead end."

"Fine, but you need to be careful too. All the clerks know you've been asking questions. We're counting on you, but be safe."

We exchanged cell phone numbers and agreed to check in after I'd talked to Thomas and Lupe.

CHAPTER TWENTY-THREE

"WHY DO THEY HAVE THESE things?"

Derek and I stood side by side in front of a mirror. I looked rather frumpy in my wrinkled black workout pants and baggy green T-shirt, while Derek looked like he'd just stepped out of a fitness magazine, slim lines and not one hair out of place.

"You want to know why mirrors exist?"

"No. I want to know why is the gym covered in them? This is the place where I'm the least likely to be presentable, and I'm reminded of it every time I see a wall."

"The mirrors help with form." Derek grabbed a loaded barbell in an overhand grip. He lifted the bar off the floor with a mighty exhale, letting it hang in front of him just above his knees.

I was holding a fifteen-pound dumbbell in each hand and attempting the same move.

"Lift with your hamstrings, not your back. You'll hurt yourself," he said. He set his burden down and stood behind me. "Put them on the ground. Now reach down and grab the weights."

I bent over; he stood beside me and placed a hand on the small of my back.

"Don't tense up. Push your hips forward and lift with your legs."

I did as he suggested and found the life much more comfortable. "Thanks, that's better."

I finished my set and returned the weights to the rack. My hands smelled like wet rust, and I wiped them on my pants. We went to the treadmills for our cool down.

I set the treadmill at 3 miles per hour and used a towel to mop the sweat from my eyes. Working out with a friend was always good. Derek had been traveling for work, and I was glad he was back in town. I was supposed to exercise while he was gone, but I'd slacked off in his absence.

Derek stretched his hands above his head and yawned. "How's the investigation going?"

"Slowly," I said. I filled him in on recent events, and told him I was going to see the family one more time, and try to discover what was behind Anna's recent windfall. He frowned when I described the missing audit sheet.

"Hold on. You found potential evidence, and when you looked into it, someone removed it?"

"Yeah."

"But that makes it sound like the murderer works there." Derek hit the button on his treadmill a few times to slow down the pace. "Did you call the police?"

"The day before yesterday," I said. "Patterson knows about the misfiles. I haven't told her about the missing audit page, I wasn't sure how to bring it up without telling her we'd been snooping around."

INVOLUNTARY TURNOVER 157

"Kat, you need to stop investigating."

"What?" I turned to look at Derek and saw he'd already stopped his treadmill. I punched the shutdown button on mine.

"Why would I do that?"

"Your coworker was murdered. You've been asking questions, and it seems she was involved in something shady. You start digging, and as soon as you do, evidence goes missing. Is that a fair summary?" Derek's eyes flashed. Was he mad at me?

"I need to be careful. But I don't think—"

Derek turned away from me, and when he turned back, he spoke in a low voice, "You don't think, Kat. That's what's scaring me. You could be in danger, and you don't think about it. Has it occurred to you that what happened to the dead woman could happen to you, too? You're a fool if—"

"Let's walk." I grabbed his elbow and dragged him toward the locker rooms, away from the crowd of gym patrons.

"First of all," I said, "you were the one who encouraged me to investigate. And second, I'm doing perfectly fine. I'm asking reasonable questions and sharing my findings with the authorities." Derek tried to interrupt, but I talked right over him. "Last but not least, there's no reason for you to talk to me like I'm a child. You're not better than me, or smarter than me, and you have no right to—."

I had more to say, but I felt hot tears land on my cheek. In a flash of anger and embarrassment, I fled into the women's locker room.

DEREK MAY HAVE WAITED OUTSIDE to continue our argument, but I never found out. I was determined to take the longest shower of my life, and if necessary, to slip outside camouflaged by a flock of yoga moms.

While the hot water washed away any outward signs of my embarrassment, inwardly I was mortified. I'd cried in front of Derek and in a public place, no less. But why was I the one who was feeling bad? This was his fault, not mine.

By the time I left the gym (checking around corners to make sure he was gone), it was late. I hurried to my car. If traffic wasn't too bad, I could get home in time to call Dori before she put the boys to bed.

I grabbed my keys out of the dusty side pocket of my gym bag and walked through the parking lot, toward my spot in the back.

I'd just unlocked my door and was about to sit down when I saw something yellow tucked underneath my driver side windshield wiper.

Had Derek left me a note? No, it was an interoffice envelope from Holy Heart. That was weird. Maybe it had fallen out of my car and someone had put it where I would see it? Only that didn't make sense either. I didn't bring interoffice mail home with me. I flipped it over to untie the string that kept the flap closed, and I saw it was addressed to human resources without a sender specified.

My heart thudded a warning, and I glanced around the parking lot. Traffic had thinned, but there was still a steady stream of cars racing by just beyond the juniper trees at the edge of the lot.

My fingers closed on a single sheet of paper. It was a blank piece of company stationary with our pale blue logo printed on the top and our street address running across the bottom. On the back of the page seven words nearly stopped my heart.

BACK OFF BITCH OR YOU DIE NEXT

CHAPTER TWENTY-FOUR

I SPUN AROUND AND PLACED my back against my car. A trio of women carrying yoga mats walked out of the gym's double doors and embraced before going their separate ways. I looked left and right, but I was alone.

After stuffing the page back in the envelope, I checked the backseat and trunk of my car. Nothing. I kneeled and looked beneath the chassis too.

Still nothing.

I eased into the car, quickly locked all four doors, and slipped the pepper spray from my purse into the cup holder to my right. I dialed the numbers nine-one-one on my cell phone and sat it on my lap, ready to hit the call button if anyone appeared.

Those precautions made, I took the page out again and reread it. The envelope was heavy; I pushed my hand all the way to the seam at the bottom. There were a few postcard sized objects in there, printed on slick paper.

I pulled out a stack of pictures that looked like they had been produced on a cheap photo printer. The one on top showed me walking into the office with Davis after the funeral.

Another was of me getting into my car in the staff parking lot. The final image made me want to jam my keys into the ignition and hurry home. It was taken from the sidewalk below my condo and showed Milo looking down from the window sill in my living room.

The message was clear. This person knew who I was, who I worked with, and where I lived. They had access to my workplace.

I picked up my phone and stared at the screen. My finger hovered over the send button. I hit the power button instead and let out a shaky exhale. I needed to think and check on my cat. Most importantly, I wanted to show whoever was watching me that their message had worked.

MILO WAS FINE. A BIT alarmed after I burst in the front door and checked him for injuries, but otherwise fine. After I scoured the condo for intruders, holding my pepper spray in one hand, I lowered my blinds and sat down on my bed to think.

A sensible person would call the police. Then they'd book a nice long vacation to Cabo and put this entire thing behind them. Why not be sensible?

Screw sensible. I strode into the living room and raised the blinds, revealing myself to the night, and then went into the kitchen to make a big pot of coffee.

I was done being threatened, insulted, and controlled. Who sent anonymous threats? Cowards and bullies, that's who. If they'd intended to kill me, they could have done so. That note was a transparent attempt to scare me off.

Why did I always let others push me around? Neil said I was too stubborn to make a good partner, but really he wanted a yes-wife to do his bidding. Angela had called me naïve, but she was a cynical ice queen who lacked empathy for anyone beneath her paygrade. Derek calling me a fool had hurt, and he was wrong too. Seeking the truth was the right thing to do.

I was done being pushed around, insulted, and intimidated, and the photo of Milo was the last straw. Insult me if you will, I thought, but no one threatens my cat.

The coffee was ready; I poured myself an extra-large cup and added cream and sugar.

Milo jumped up on the counter, jonesing for an ear-scratch. I obliged.

"I'm done being bullied," I told him. "And I'm going to figure out who this sonofabitch is."

Milo chirped his approval. Leaving him devouring a bowl full of canned food, I went down to the lobby to talk to our security guard.

"Hey there." I placed my hands on the reception desk and leaned forward, glimpsing a peek of his magazine, which featured muscled men in a variety of poses, gleaming with oil.

"Workout magazines," he muttered, pushing it underneath his clipboard. "What can I do for you, Ms. Voyzey?"

"I need to change my elevator security code please."

He pulled out a pin pad for me to type into. "Is everything all right?" he asked.

"Everything's fine," I lied. "I realized my old code is easy to break, and there is this creep that I dated who knows it. I haven't seen him in months, but just in case, don't send anyone up to my floor, okay? If I get deliveries, I'll come down and pick them up myself."

"Sure, I'll make a note in the system. Need anything else?"

"Nope. Good luck with your workouts."

His ears turned pink, and he nodded.

NOW THAT MY HOME WAS marginally more secure, I needed to take a few steps to minimize my risks at work. Most of them were easy, but one of them was going to piss my new friends in medical records off. Unfortunately, there was no way around it.

First, I left for work thirty minutes later than usual. That way I wouldn't be alone when I walked in from the parking garage. By that time the employee lot was getting busy, and I was able to follow a few other employees all the way inside.

Second, I spent all morning showing off how I'd left the investigation behind. In fact, I was a model of productivity. I answered phone calls, sent off expense reports, and helped Erin update our training schedule for the following six months. I avoided the lower level of the hospital at all costs.

My next maneuver would be the most difficult, and probably the most unpleasant.

At one fifteen, I went to the cafeteria to put on a show. Sally and Bridget were eating lunch before their shifts started, and luckily, they were sitting at the center of the room.

Good. The bigger the audience the better.

I bought soup from the hot food line and walked over to the condiment station near their table to get a spoon and napkins. As expected, they saw me and waved me over.

"Hey, Kat." Sally said. "Want to join us?"

"Any news in the investigation?" Bridget asked.

I resisted the urge to look around and see who was watching. Instead, I went into full-on HR mode.

"Ladies, I've been thinking. It was inappropriate of me to ask you two to get involved in what is clearly none of our business. We need to stop violating company policy, and we need to let the police do their jobs without our interference."

Sally furrowed her brow. "But we talked about this. We want to help. And you didn't talk us into anything."

"You mean well, but I wouldn't want anyone to get hurt," I emphasized the word 'hurt', hoping they'd take the hint. "Anna is gone, and I think it's best we find a way to accept it and move on."

Bridget raised her eyebrows. Sally's eyes narrowed, and she looked ready to argue.

I shook my head. "I'm sorry, but no more investigating. This isn't up for debate; I'm telling you to stop." I looked at my watch. "And I need to get back to work."

Holding my soup in both hands, I walked away.

Bridget and Sally might hate me now, but it was better to be disappointed than dead.

I sat at my desk with the door open, drank my soup, and made sure everyone could see me working on a spreadsheet. And when a call came in from medical records at five p.m., I didn't pick up the phone. Whoever was calling didn't leave a message, but I hoped they'd received mine.

CHAPTER TWENTY-FIVE

I WANTED A BURNER PHONE. That sounds terribly CSI of me, but I wasn't sure how the murderer had been tracking my activities. My office phone might be monitored, the hospital had recording of software for 'quality control purposes' and I wasn't sure who had access.

Also, it seemed safer not to use my personal cell phone. My brother-in-law was always telling me how moronically simple it was to hack into phones and computers. "Never open a file from an unknown source," he'd told me. "They can install a keylogger on your smartphone or computer and gain access to all your stuff."

If a murderer was bold enough to follow me to work and the gym, why not bug my communications? It would be the easiest way to track me.

While Jocelyn was at lunch, I used her terminal to research how to buy a prepaid phone. All I needed to do was buy a disposable phone and prepaid card at a convenience store, pay cash, and then provide bogus information on the registration page.

One trip to the drug store later to pick up "snacks for the break room," and I was all set.

My personal cell phone was on silent, due to the number of people I was avoiding. Derek had sent me an apology text, but I ignored it. Sally left me a message asking what the hell was going on, and I didn't reply to that either.

Instead I closed my office door and dialed Thomas.

"Vasquez residence, this is Beth."

"This is Kat Voyzey calling for Thomas."

There was a blank space on the line. "You're from Mama's work. Her friends from work said you're helping the police."

"I was," I said. "Have the police found anything helpful?"

"They searched the house, and they left with money they found. That's all I know."

That wasn't good, but I didn't say so out loud.

"The police are wrong about my mother, but they'll figure it out," Beth said. "When I was using, I knew not to call home because she'd tell me to go to rehab. And I didn't come by because she'd call the cops."

"What will you do now? Are you staying here in Seattle?"

"I hope so. Thomas found me an attorney and I start treatment soon. It's what she would have wanted."

"Good luck to you. I know she'd be proud."

"Thank you. I'll get my uncle on the phone."

I heard a click, and a shuffling noise. "Kat, thank you for calling. Do you have any news for us?"

"I've done a little digging, but I'm afraid it only raised more questions. Your sister never received a promotion. She told one coworker that she had a 'side job' and that she was earning money to send the kids to a private school by selling something. I was hoping you might have found something in her personal effects, perhaps a clue as to what she was doing."

Thomas grunted. "The police found a large sum of cash in her bedroom. They took it as evidence, but they did not say what it was evidence of."

"Have you uncovered anything else that might shed light on her side job? Paperwork, perhaps? An employment contract?"

"No," he said. "We're as confused by it as you are. My sister never lied to us before."

Legitimate employers didn't pay their employees in untraceable cash. I wondered if he knew, but I didn't bring it up.

"I'm glad Beth is home. Is she well?" I doubted Lupe and Thomas would allow her to see the children if she was still doing drugs, but she'd seemed so shaky at the funeral.

"It is a miracle," Thomas said, and I could hear the pride in his voice. "She's talking to a counselor every day and working very hard. If she continues to do well, we hope to share custody of the children. It seems Anna's prayers have been answered at last. I only wish she was here to see it."

"That's wonderful news," I said. "And I'm sorry that I don't have better news about the investigation. Do you need anything else from us?"

"Hold on. We have a question about my sister's life insurance." Papers rustled in the background. "Seattle Life & Casualty."

"That policy isn't one of ours. Do they have a hotline?"

"They do, but it was busy. I'll try it again. And please call if you hear anything else from Anna's friends at work. I know this doesn't look good, but I'm still holding out hope. I refuse to believe my sister was a criminal."

"I'm not giving up either," I said. "Do me a favor. I'm wondering if you recognize any of these names." Moving down the list Sally had given me, I read aloud the names of the dead patients whose charts had been misfiled.

"No, none of those sound familiar. Does it matter?"

"No, it was a long shot. Thanks for your help. If you could do me a favor, please don't tell anyone that I'm asking questions. It could get me into a lot of trouble with my boss."

"I won't say a word," he promised. "But please be careful. We don't want you to get in any trouble, either. We're grateful that you and her friends care so much, but nothing we do will bring my sister back."

CHAPTER TWENTY-SIX

I REMAINED VIGILANT INTO THE evening, leaving the office with a large group of employees just after five p.m. and monitoring the space around and behind myself as I moved.

All was quiet as I went to bed that night, but I couldn't breathe a sigh of relief. Not yet. I'd worked hard to escape the murderer's notice, but my investigation had come to a grinding halt as a result. Sleep came easily, but I woke up feeling weary, as if none of my rest had counted.

The next morning was dark. Seattle was buried under a thick blanket of gray clouds and not even a peep of sunlight was coming through. Once I was in my office, I pulled out the list of dead patient names and unfolded the page, scrutinizing the tidy black handwriting. I refolded it along the well-worn creases in the paper.

Why couldn't I let this go? The police had a theory that the facts almost fit. I couldn't explain the cash they'd recovered at Anna's house, or the many ways she'd lied about where it came from. Hell, the threatening note on my car probably came from her supplier.

The sensible thing would be to give the note to the cops, back the heck up, and stay out of their way. But the official theory didn't explain the misfiles, or why Anna would get into the drug business to start with.

If you have a puzzle and you cram the pieces into a messy picture, do you call it done? Not if there were pieces left over! We were missing something, and I needed to find it. But how?

Erin knocked on my door and opened it without waiting for me to reply. I slid the square of paper into my pocket.

"Are you trying to live like a bat?" Erin was holding an armful of three ring binders.

"What?" Erin has one of those minds that jumps from one topic to the next without warning. This time I hadn't made the leap.

"It's dark in here, like a cave. And I can hear your little desk fountain running, like water dripping. Plus, you are wearing mostly black." She was right. I hadn't realized it, but my attempt to lie low had influenced my wardrobe.

"True," I said. "Give me a few more days, and you'll find me hanging from the ceiling by my toes." Erin set her load of binders down on one chair and sat in the other.

"We need a new copy machine," She announced, holding out a binder and flipping the white plastic cover open. "See those smudges on the pages and those grainy dots at the bottom? That happens every time. We're supposed to be running a world class training program, but it looks like we copy our materials at a roadside gas station."

"Have you called Todd?"

"Yes, once a month for the last six months. He says our machine is too old to fix. We need a new one."

"I'll look into it, but it's not in this year's budget."

Erin rolled her eyes. "You know who has a shiny new copier? The pediatrics department. They make, like, ten copies a day, and they have the best equipment. But we're HR, a lousy admin department, so we get the machine that looks like—"

"—one from a roadside gas station."

"Exactly."

"I feel your pain, friend, but watch this." I dialed a number on speakerphone.

A gruff male voice answered, "Facilities, this is Joe."

"Hey Joe, it's Kat and Erin from HR. We have a question about our copier."

"The maintenance number is on the side. If you call them, they'll—"

"Erin has had them out already, and they can always fix our copier temporarily. The trouble is that it's ancient, and our copies look like garbage. When are we due to get a new copier?"

Joe grunted and asked us to hold. Less than a minute later, he was back.

"Three years," he said.

Erin groaned. "What happens if we want a new copier sooner?"

"Nothing," he said. "If it breaks, the coper company has to fix it."

"And if the fixes don't work?" Erin said.

"They'll fix it as many times as it takes," Joe said. I heard a squeak as his chair protested under his frame. "Here's the deal, ladies. We lease these copiers. It's like a car. You're stuck with it until the lease expires. Even if we gave it back, we'd still have to pay for it for the next three years. That's why the hospital won't give you a new one before three years is up."

Erin said, "Well, that's fucking stupid."

Joe laughed out loud. I nudged Erin with my foot and shook my head. "We hear you Joe. But between you and me, is there a loophole?"

"Maybe if it's stolen? I'm sorry I don't have better news."

"Thanks Joe." I hung up the phone and looked over at Erin who was eyeing the keys on my desk.

"You're not stealing the copier."

"But if it went missing one night—"

"Give me one of those binders," I said. "I'll show it to Angela and tell her we're the laughingstock of the training world. Perhaps the horror of not being excellent will spur her into action."

"And if that doesn't work?"

I shrugged. "Hey. All I'm saying is that I'm not bailing you out of jail if you get caught."

"Are you two busy?" Jocelyn was at the door holding a document. "I finished all those criminal background checks you asked for."

"Anything we should worry about?"

She shook her head. "Nope, thank goodness. No criminals of any stripe. Wait. Isn't that good news? You look disappointed."

It was good news, but it also meant that I'd reached another dead end.

CHAPTER TWENTY-SEVEN

"ARE YOU LOOKING FOR SOMEONE?" a gentle male voice asked.

Father Callahan was holding two cups of coffee. He sat next to me on the bench and handed me one.

"Maybe," I said, and thanked him for the beverage. I'd been hoping to run into Shelby, but I didn't want to wander down to the medical records department while I might be under surveillance. That's why I was sitting at the feet of Sister Constance's statue, checking email on my phone.

"I'm glad I ran into you," He said. "It's been a frightening time for the staff. It seems the police believe one thing, and the hearts of the people believe another."

I nodded.

"How are you holding up? I hear you've been serving the team, trying to help."

Glancing sideways, I wondered who he'd been speaking to. And if he'd sought me out by accident or by design.

"I'm fine, thank you. Can I ask you a question?"

"Please do."

"I'm curious, Father. How do you maintain faith when all available evidence points the other way?"

"I take it this isn't a biblical question?" He raised an eyebrow and took a sip from his coffee.

"You know it isn't."

He set his cup down, freeing his hands so he could gesture as he spoke. "You ask a fundamental question. *The* question, some might say. Where does faith come from, and how do we reconcile it with the flesh-and-blood world?

"Faith is the most radical of the Christian principles. Charity, humility, and good works: we can see the results, the evidence, you might say. But faith comes from in here." He tapped his sternum with two fingers.

"So what is a person supposed to do, when they believe one thing, but the evidence says something else?"

He tapped his chest one more time and smiled. "You listen! You act in accordance with what you know is right, and you allow for the possibility of miracles."

"I don't know if I believe in miracles. In fact, I'm pretty sure I don't."

"Ah, but how could you not, when you're surrounded by them?"

I sighed inwardly. Father Callahan meant well, but he and I didn't speak the same language.

"Ah, I see you're skeptical. But think on this: Anna may have gone to heaven too soon, and we miss her, but in doing so, her daughter is returned to the path of righteousness. And here I am, getting my caffeine fix, when I discover Kat Voyzey at the foot of Sister Constance, seeking the truth."

"You've got a very low bar for miracles, Father." I worried that I might offend him, but he only chuckled.

"Perhaps. But remember, our hospital was built upon the insistence of a woman who persevered, and who wasn't afraid to break with custom to achieve a higher purpose. I see Sister Constance's spirit in you, and it's no accident that I found you here today." He stood and held up his coffee cup. "The coffee here is good, isn't it? I should get back to my duties. I'll see you later."

I waved goodbye, unsure what to make of what he'd said. As soon as the Father was out of sight, I glimpsed Shelby walking by with an armful of files.

"Hey," I said. "Do you have a minute? I have a management question."

She nodded and slowed her steps, I walked alongside her. There was a bloom of acne on her chin and she looked exhausted. Had something else happened?

My plan was to break the ice with a work question, and then pivot to asking her about the missing page from the audit book. Shelby had access to the department after hours, and I couldn't exclude her from scrutiny. If she reacted nervously to my questions, it might tell me something.

"Say, I heard you're dating one of our vendors," I said, keeping my tone casual. "It's no biggie, but I wanted to talk about restructuring our contract with them to avoid any conflict of interest."

Shelby burst into tears, and I pulled her into a quiet hallway nearby. "Oh no. What did I say? You're not in trouble! It's just a paperwork thing; we can't have you signing time sheets for your boyfriend."

"I don't have a boyfriend," Shelby said, wiping her nose with her sleeve. "We broke up this morning. He sent me a text message, can you believe that? What are we, twelve?"

"Oh, hon. I'm so sorry. How long were you together?"

"Six months. He's moving to Portland, and he doesn't want to do long distance so he's 'setting me free'. Like I'm a bird or something."

"I handed her a tissue from my purse, she unfolded it and blotted her eyes."

"He was all set to meet my parents over Thanksgiving. Now they'll act like it was my fault."

"Ugh, I can relate. When I got dumped a year ago, my sister cross-examined me, looking for my mistake."

Shelby wiped her eyes. "It's not just me then."

"That's why I'm taking a break from romance. Friends are better than boyfriends, no drama required." I thought about Derek's text message, which I still hadn't returned, and felt a pang of guilt. Giving him the cold shoulder wasn't fair. How would I feel if our situations were reversed?

"No drama sounds great to me." Shelby used her fingers to smooth her hair back into a ponytail. "God, I want this year to be over. The breakup isn't even the worst of it. I keep thinking about Anna and feeling like it's my fault."

"Why would it be your fault?"

"She wanted to get out of her shift, but I said no. I told her she couldn't volunteer to work and pull out when it got inconvenient for her."

"That sounds reasonable. You couldn't have known what would happen."

"I'd gotten it into my head that my staff were walking all over me, taking advantage. If it wasn't for me feeling superior, she might still be alive."

"You did nothing wrong."

"Yeah." Shelby dropped her head.

"Did she say why she wanted the night off?"

"No, just that she had things to do."

"Shelby?"

"Yeah."

"Have you heard anything about a missing page in your audit book?"

She looked up. "Amy mentioned it, and it's not that big of a deal. Why? Is it important?"

"I'm grasping at straws, I guess. Trying to find information to help the police figure out what happened."

Shelby's eyes narrowed. "Well, I'd love to nail whoever did this to a wall. If I can help, let me know."

"Will do. And let me know if you ever need to vent, I'm around."

"Thanks." She shook her head and stood up straighter. "He's not worth the tears. A text message? What a jerk. Why can't I meet a nice guy? Someone who just treats me like... a person, you know?"

"He's out there," I said, touching her arm. "Sometimes you need to kiss a few frogs to find the right one. At least that's what they say."

I pulled out my phone as I walked back to my office. It was time to call Derek and apologize.

"I'M SORRY," I BLURTED OUT, as soon as he picked up the line. "I'm sorry that I flipped out, and I was a jerk for not returning your messages. You were only thinking about my safety. Please forgive me."

There was a pause, and a familiar buzzing noise on the line. My stomach lurched. Was I on speakerphone?

"Kat? Is that you?" In the background I heard shuffling papers and the distant sound of someone unfamiliar clearing their throat.

"Um. Did I catch you at a bad time?"

"I'll call you back in ten minutes."

Lowering my head to my desk, I thumped my forehead on the surface three times. When I sat up, there was a yellow sticky note affixed to my forehead; I pulled it off and read it. Detective Patterson had left me a message, asking me to call back.

When my phone finally rang, I answered it. "Holy Heart human resources, this is Kat, how can I help you?"

"It's me," Derek said.

"Did you hear that?"

"Did I hear what?"

"The way I introduced myself when I answered the phone. You know, a proper phone greeting, so you didn't launch into a speech in the middle of someone else's meeting."

He laughed. "Yes, but it's not my fault! You dialed my work phone, not my cell. I was expecting a call, so I'd forwarded it to the conference room."

"How embarrassed were you?"

"At first, quite a bit."

"But then you realized you forgave me, so all was well?"

"Sure. Also, the client in the room with me thought it was hilarious; he was in a great mood for the rest of our meeting. So it all worked out."

"I'm sorry about our fight," I said.

"You don't need to be. I was the one being an ass. I should have said I was afraid you'd get hurt, but instead I acted like a jerk."

"I was a jerk too."

"Not really."

"So, we're good?

I heard the smile in his voice as he answered. "Yes, we're good. Say, I want to hear what you've been up to. Thai takeout at your place?"

"Saturday night?"

"Seven?"

Someone rapped on my door, twice. "See you then," I said to Derek, before hanging up. When I looked up, Susan Patterson was standing in my doorway.

"Can I borrow you?" she asked.

"Sure. Why?"

"I want to talk to Dr. Carter, and I figured you could introduce us."

CHAPTER TWENTY-EIGHT

"YOU'VE BEEN BUSY," DETECTIVE PATTERSON said.

"Detective—"

"Call me Susan,"

"I don't know what you heard, but all I've done is ask questions. The clerks aren't satisfied with where things stand, neither is the family, and to be honest neither am I."

"Yes. You've not exactly been subtle."

"Wait, I—"

"It's an observation, not an insult. But I don't give up as easily as you believe. The evidence against Ms. Vasquez was damning, but that's the problem."

"What?"

Susan smirked at me. "Small time drug dealers don't hold that much product, or that much cash. Distributors have infrastructure: networks, connections, and regular supply drops. Ms. Vasquez was holding too much to be a small fry, and we've found zero evidence she's connected to anything bigger."

"The evidence doesn't add up."

"That's an understatement. If it was a break-in, why didn't they take anything? And if your coworker was a drug dealer why is there no evidence of activity? The cash has me wondering though. There's no sign it was planted, and there's plenty of it."

"Why are you telling me this?" I asked.

"Because every time I talk to someone, I discover you've been there first. This isn't how I like to do things, but you're annoyingly persistent. Besides, people around here seem to trust you, and I figure if I bring you along, it might loosen a few tongues."

"Anna requested to work the night shift the day she died, but she tried to get out of it at the last minute," I said.

"That feeds into a theory of mine." She pulled a small notepad out of her pocket and flipped to the page she was looking for. "Bridget Chan went to the cafeteria. Then our victim tells her other coworker, Sally Jacobs, that Dr. Carter needs some files urgently."

"You think Anna was trying to get her coworkers out of there."

"It's possible. That's why I want to talk to the doctor, to see if he did in fact request those records."

"That's easy, but we should talk to his medical assistant." I said, pointing at the phone. "May I?"

She nodded, and I dialed the doctor's medical assistant. When he answered, I asked him to look in the computer and verify the request.

"I don't need to look," he said. "I can tell you it didn't happen."

"How do you know?"

"Doctor C was on vacation."

"So he didn't request any patient files Halloween night."

"Not unless he did so from Hawaii."

Susan signaled me and whispered something. I nodded and put the phone back to my ear.

"What happens to medical records if they're dropped off when the doctor isn't there?"

"They're delivered to the nursing station. Anything not picked up is returned to medical records at the start of the next shift."

I thanked him and hung up the phone. "Doctor Carter was on vacation and didn't request the charts. And Sally wouldn't have known it was a ruse because the files are left at the nursing station."

"Anna wanted her coworkers out of the department."

"And she tried to get out of working that night."

"Was she avoiding someone?" I wondered aloud. "And did she know she was in danger?"

Susan paced the open area in my office. "We're getting closer to the truth; I can feel it."

I thought of the list in my pocket and wondered if I should tell Susan. My rational-brain said yes. But I didn't want to get Bridget and Sally fired, or myself for that matter. Could I trust her?

"What is it?" she asked.

"Let's say I had information, but I might have violated company policy to get it. Hypothetically."

"Is this a corporate nonsense thing? Because we're dealing with a serious crime and keeping information from me is obstruction."

"No, I'll tell you. It's just that I bent the company rules to get this information, and I'd rather not get my sources fired."

Susan nodded. "Understood. What's the lead?"

"Remember how I told you about misfiled records, the morning after the murder? I thought your guys might have done it."

"Yes. I followed up, and one of the clerks said they put them all back and it was no big deal."

"What if I told you I got a list of the misfiles, and they were all for dead people?"

Susan's eyebrows shot up, and she smiled, showing perfect white teeth. "Is that a fact? Did they die of similar causes, any violent—"

"Nope. Ordinary deaths; mostly they were elderly and sick. Nothing remarkable about them, but it looks like Anna requested those charts from our storage facility. I tried finding a connection between them, online, but no luck."

"You know, this would have been useful information for me to have. I've been spinning my wheels for days."

"Well, I told you several things. And it's not like you guys have seemed interested in what we have to say."

She sighed. "That's fair. Have you talked to any of them yet?"

"The dead people?"

"No, smartass. Their families. Perhaps they knew our victim."

"Really?"

She shrugged her shoulders. As her suit jacket shifted, I caught a glimpse of her service pistol in its holster. "I'll take those names." She glanced at her watch. "Evans and I can canvas them tomorrow. It's a Saturday, we may be able to catch people at home."

"I'll give you the names, but only if you take me along."

"No way. You're persistent, I'll give you that. But this is police business."

"And it's my list. Besides, you said people trust me; maybe I can help. And if we run into someone connected with the hospital, wouldn't you want someone who could tell you? I know everyone who works here." This was a slight exaggeration, but she didn't need to know that.

She regarded me, brown eyes meeting green ones, but when she grinned, I knew that I'd won her over.

"Fine. Lord knows you'd probably get in my way if I don't keep an eye on you. Give me the list so I can check it over tonight, and I'll meet you tomorrow at ten a.m. at Cyberdogs."

"Are you sure you don't want to meet at a donut shop?" I spit out the joke without thinking, but I immediately worried that I'd gone too far.

Susan laughed, then pointed at me with one index finger. "Watch it, or I'll make you ride in the backseat."

"YOU'RE SMILING," JOCELYN SAID, AS she tidied up the lobby, stacking magazines and pushing chairs into alignment. "Are you feeling better?"

"I guess I am," I said.

I mentally ran through my behavior for the prior week. I'd been hiding out in my office with the door shut, making strange information requests, and disappearing for hours at a time. My team had been dealing with a moody and unpredictable manager for a while now, and I hadn't even noticed.

"I'm sorry I've been acting weird lately," I said. "I'll try to be more normal."

"Well, not too normal," Jocelyn said. "You wouldn't fit in here otherwise."

I asked her about her weekend plans, and she told me that her boyfriend was taking her to the Ballard Locks for a date. "He says they open the gates to raise or lower the amount of water, so the boats can get through. It's interesting."

My doubt must have shown because she laughed. "Okay! I admit it! Phil thinks it's interesting. And I don't much care what we do because I enjoy spending time with him."

I remembered that feeling. When you're with someone you care about, dates and dinners are just an excuse to be in the same location for a while. I nodded. "That's the best, isn't it? Like when I go to the gym with Derek. I hate working out, but when he's there, it's fun."

"Precisely. Should we lock up? Everyone else is already gone. Akiko had her thing."

"What thing?"

"She didn't tell you? Her *World of Warcraft* group is in a tournament this weekend. It's a big deal—if they win they get ten-thousand dollars. And a magic sword or something? I don't really understand how it works."

"Me either, but that sounds cool. And it fits her. I've always thought of Akiko as the warrior type."

Joss clapped her hands. "That's it! Let's make her a sword! I've got wrapping paper tubes and glitter at home, and we can give it to her at the staff meeting. She's been working so hard lately. What do you say?"

"Best idea ever," I said. "I'll bring snacks."

Derek and I were friends again, the murder investigation was moving forward, and my team was the best I could ask for. On the way home from work I turned the radio up and sang my heart out.

CHAPTER TWENTY-NINE

TUCKED UNDER THE MASSIVE CONCRETE facade of the Washington State Convention Center, there's a tiny cafe as dark as a cave. CyberDogs serves up both hot dogs and internet by the hour, so I ordered myself a spudnik (a hot dog with spiced potatoes and scallions) and carried it over to the nearest unoccupied terminal.

Awake since seven and fueled by a pot and a half of coffee, I arrived early for my rendezvous with Susan, figuring I could use the extra time to find addresses for our canvas. It was slow going, but by cross-referencing the names of family members (found in obituaries) with property tax records for the county, I was making progress.

Edwin Hunter (beloved father, husband, and high school history teacher) had passed away peacefully after a long illness. I found his wife's address online.

Marybelle Lewis died from complications of breast cancer just two months ago. Her daughter's contact information was on Facebook. She hadn't bothered to make her profile private, fortunately for me.

Simone Cutbert had no obituary listed, but I found a listing for Josh and Simone Cutbert on Beacon Hill. I wrote down their address and phone number.

Joe Campos and Stuart Yates had died over a year ago. I found several potential numbers for Mr. Yates's family home, but Joe Campos did not have any information listed online. There were dozens of men named Campos in the greater Seattle area, but no one named Joe. Perhaps it was a nickname?

Someone tapped me on the shoulder; it was Susan. She was carrying a bag from Top Pot Doughnuts, but as I wasn't sure if she was being ironic, I didn't bring it up.

"You ready to go?" She glanced at my scribbled notes and the open web browser. "What are you doing?"

"Researching our leads," I said. "I've found a couple addresses, but not all of them."

Susan shook her head. "I've done that already. DMV records, remember? We're good to go. I'll order coffee then we can get rolling."

She bought two coffees and handed me one, I tossed my empty in the trash and followed her to the parking garage, stretching my legs to keep up. She wasn't much taller than me, but she moved fast.

"Who are we seeing first?" I asked.

"Patrice Hunter. She lives at a retirement community in upper Queen Anne."

"Is your partner coming with us?" I wasn't the biggest fan of Detective Evans, but I assumed detectives always worked in pairs.

"No, we're spread a bit thin. He's working another case today."

The Miraflores retirement apartments were shabby on the outside, with flaking paint and a neglected lawn. But the interior was comfortably furnished and spotless.

We passed through the automatic doors and approached the counter. Susan flashed her badge and told the receptionist who we wanted to see.

"Room two oh four," she said. "Down the second hallway, and knock loud, she's a little deaf."

Susan followed those instructions, and after a hesitant reply from the occupant, we entered the small apartment.

A slight-figured woman was sitting in a recliner with knitting gear in her lap; she looked at us with an expression of welcome, but it quickly melted into something like annoyance.

"You're not Trixie. What do you two want? I already get the Seattle Times on my iPad, and I don't need any dishwasher warranties."

Susan stepped forward while keeping a respectful distance. "I'm Detective Patterson from the Seattle Police Department. We'd like to ask you a few questions about your late husband."

Mrs. Hunter picked up the reading glasses she wore on a chain around her neck and placed them on her nose, peering at us. "If this is one of those scams against the elderly, you're not getting anything from me. My son-in-law does my finances.

"Go hassle the women in the television room. They think the Kardashians are the height of sophistication, perhaps you'll have more luck with them."

"She's not lying," I said. "Do you want to see her badge?"

Mrs. Hunter looked at me, skeptical, and then nodded. Susan held out her badge for inspection.

"Well, what's this got to do with Ed?"

"Probably nothing," Susan said, sitting down on the unoccupied couch. I did the same. "I'm investigating a shooting that took place at Holy Heart. Your husband's medical record was found at the crime scene."

"And?"

"We're checking a few things off our list. Can I read some names to you? I'm wondering if you know any of these people."

She assented.

Susan read off the names, slowly, and waited for a flicker of recognition in Ms. Hunter's eyes. There was only impatience.

"I don't know those people."

Susan handed her a photo of Anna and asked if she recognized her.

"No. Never seen her in my life."

"Was there anything unusual with your husband's passing?" I asked.

"Unusual? No. He'd been ill for years—congestive heart failure—and it was a matter of time. He was a fighter. Lasted longer than anyone expected him to." Her expression softened at the memory, and she fingered the wedding ring she still wore.

"Did he have any new friends or business acquaintances in the year prior to his death?" Susan asked.

She thought for a moment. "No, not that I can think of. Most of our friends were from the church—that's St. Stephens. And we've been retired for thirty years."

Susan asked a few more questions, but none of them prompted any useful information. She provided a copy of her card and asked Ms. Hunter to call if she thought of anything else, and we returned to her vehicle.

"Well, that wasn't helpful," I said.

She nodded. "On television, the cops go from one lucky break to another. It's not like that in real life."

"So, we continue?"

"Exactly."

Our next two stops were a bust. The first turned out to be an incorrect address, and at the second, no one was home. "We'll come back if we have time," Susan said.

After checking her list, Susan drove us to the Beacon Hill neighborhood on the south side of the city. Formerly known for its gang violence and frequent car break-ins, an influx of wealthy tech employees had gentrified the area, resulting in less crime but unaffordable rents for many of the former residents.

We pulled up in front of a small brick rambler. The yard was tiny but newly mowed, and the bright white trim around the windows looked freshly painted. I knocked twice on the heavy wooden door and a handsome older man opened it.

"Oh my," he said, his eyes widening when he saw Susan's car parked at the curb. "Have you come to arrest me?"

CHAPTER THIRTY

JOSH CUTBERT LISTENED TO OUR story with interest and offered to brew us coffee while Susan explained our task. "I've got the good stuff, none of that Starbucks schlock," he said.

Never one to turn down coffee, I agreed; Susan asked for a glass of water. While our host puttered in the kitchen, pulling mugs and plates out of cabinets, I looked around. Almost every wall of his home was covered in bookshelves, and they were overflowing. Histories and biographies mostly, but also romances and science fiction and comic books.

"You've got an impressive collection," I said.

"I was a professor, back when books were made of paper instead of pixels. My wife was an avid reader, most of the fiction is hers. Now that she's gone, I'm making my way through her books. It's a way of connecting with her I suppose."

He handed me a cup. I took a sip and sighed with happiness. This was quality.

"You don't normally get the good stuff, I take it." He grinned. "That's Stumptown. If you like it, I'll give you a list of others to try."

I wasn't sure if he was avoiding the subject of our visit or merely eager for company, but Susan seemed inclined to let the conversation wander, so I rolled with it. Only after we all had drinks and he'd set out a plate of cookies on the table did he get to the point.

"You found my wife's medical record at a crime scene. But you say the crime scene was a medical records department. Are you visiting everyone who had a file there? That seems like an odd way to spend your Saturday."

I shook my head. "Your wife's file was one of a small number that were in an unusual place. We suspect the murder victim pulled those files on purpose, and every file was from a patient who was deceased."

His eyes lit up. "Ah! Well that's a mystery, isn't it! And I'd spin a tale about foul play, but my wife died of breast cancer. It was all perfectly natural, as life and death goes. Did all the files belong to cancer patients?"

"No, there were many causes of death. All natural."

"Did they have the same doctor?"

I shook my head.

"And you're sure this is significant, somehow?"

"No, we're not," Susan said. "But it's an angle worth pursuing."

"I see," he said. "And here's another mystery. Detective Patterson here is clearly a member of the police force. But you're not." He pointed at me. "Is this some sort of trick? I want to make sure I'm not—what's the phrase young people use—being punked?"

I laughed. "No, I work at the hospital."

"Ah! You're an attorney?"

"I'm from human resources."

He looked confused, which was understandable.

"The woman who died was one of our people," I said. "Her coworkers and I wanted to help, to make sure her killer is brought to justice."

"Well, that's very hands-on of you."

"Tell me about it," Susan muttered.

"Mr. Cutburt—" I said.

"Josh."

"We know we're on a fishing expedition here," I said. I told him about Anna, her mysterious windfall, and the files that were found shoved into the stacks after her death. "We're looking for a connection. She might have gotten involved in something illegal, we just don't know what that thing is."

I glanced at Susan, wondering if I was over sharing, but she seemed content to listen. Meanwhile, Josh looked like he was trying to remember something.

"I might have what you're after," he said. He left the room and returned with a battered file folder. "Take a look at this."

Susan opened it, and I scooted my chair over so I could see what was inside.

There was a death certificate for Simone Cutbert, specifying complications from cancer as the cause of death. There were photocopies of her medical record, a few insurance certificates, and an obituary notice. Also a photo of a fit woman in her sixties standing on a hiking trail. She was smiling broadly and holding onto a pair of trekking poles while a waterfall glittered in the background.

"Is this her?" I asked gently.

"Yes. Simone and I were married for forty-two years. It's still hard to believe she's gone, but I'm glad it happened the way it did. She always told me she wanted to die in her sleep, and that's the way she went."

Josh picked up the photo. "One of the things they don't tell you about the end of life is how much damn paperwork there is. It took months. Not only getting the death certificate, but dealing with all the medical bills. Simone was very diligent about her filing, but it's been difficult to get everything organized. I was able to close out everything except this." He pointed at one of the insurance certificates.

"Seattle Life and Casualty," Susan read from the page, and slid it over to me. It was a term life insurance certificate for five hundred thousand dollars. Why did that sound familiar?

"I called them when Simone passed away, and they took my information down and said they'd send a representative to the house within forty-eight hours. They never showed, and when I tried them again, the number was disconnected."

"When did you buy this policy?" I asked.

"She purchased it a couple months before she passed."

Susan and I exchanged a meaningful look. No insurance broker in their right mind would issue a policy for half a million bucks to a dying woman. I was trying to come up with a gentle way of breaking the news to Josh when I caught him smiling at me.

"Don't worry about sparing my feelings, dear. This policy stinks like an old fish; I'm not under any illusions. Simone spent her own money on this, and she didn't tell me until it was over and done with. She wanted to take care of me, in her own way. Always an optimist, my gal."

"How much did she spend?" Susan asked.

"Three thousand dollars."

"Ouch," I said.

"I found the transaction after the funeral, when closing her accounts. She went to the bank and got a cashier's check."

I looked at Susan, "What are the odds this insurance company actually exists?"

She shook her head. "Nil. I've heard about these types of scams, but I didn't know they were operating locally."

"Mr. Cutbert, you should file a report with the attorney general. I'll give you the number." She pulled out her notepad and wrote down a name and a string of digits. "When you call, ask for Henry Shuck. He's a friend of mine, and he'll give you a case number. That will help you get your wife's money back, should it be recovered."

"Thank you. Do you think this has anything to do with your investigation?"

"Possibly," I said, my heart heavy. If Anna was selling fake insurance policies, how was it any better than dealing drugs? Either way it added up to illegal activity and taking advantage of people who were in a terrible position.

"You're disappointed," he said.

"A little. The woman who was murdered has friends and family who looked up to her. If she was selling these fake policies, she wasn't the person we thought we was."

"Hold on," Susan said. "One step at a time. What can you tell me about the person who sold your wife the policy?"

"I wasn't home when he came by. But she described him as an extremely polite young man."

"A man?" I said, perking up. "And when you called the phone number, was it a man or a woman that answered?"

"A man."

"What do you think she meant by young?" Susan asked. "Did she give you any sort of description?"

"Not exactly, but she said that he reminded her of our oldest son, Jerry." He walked over to a photograph and pointed at a young man with curly brown hair and freckles. Susan looked at me, and I shrugged.

"Did you get a name?" Susan asked.

"No. She told me about the policy when she went into the hospital for the last time. Simone told me not to spend the whole thing on strippers." Josh smiled at the memory, but I could tell remembering was painful. I felt guilty about triggering those feelings, but Susan plowed forward.

"Did your wife ever mention another person associated with the insurance policy? A woman perhaps?"

"No."

"You said he came by while Simone was home. Do you know how they got her information?"

Josh's expression brightened. "I do! Or at least I know what he claimed. He told her it was a special program through the hospital. And because she was a high-risk patient, the premiums would be high for the first year, but then reduced afterward."

A thrill of excitement shot through me. I glanced at Susan, and from the spark in her eyes she seemed to be having a similar reaction. Here was the connection to Holy Heart we'd been looking for.

"I'm going to take these insurance documents as evidence, but I'll return certified copies for your records," Susan said.

"Well, I'm glad something good has come out of this whole mess," he said.

"Me too," I said. "Although I hate that someone took advantage of your wife like this."

"Bah," he waved his hands, "I've always wanted to help solve a real murder-mystery. And you two make mighty fine company. Say, do you want another cup of coffee before you go?"

I wanted nothing more than to talk to Susan about what we'd just heard, but Josh was hard to say no to, and he was already grinding a fresh batch of beans in the kitchen.

"One more cup," I said.

CHAPTER THIRTY-ONE

SUSAN PULLED THE DOOR TO her patrol car shut, and then pulled her seatbelt across her body, latching it in place.

"Are you thinking what I'm thinking?" I asked.

"I'm thinking you've had so much caffeine your head might pop off."

"Lightweight," I teased. "I think I know where Anna was getting her cash."

"Commissions," Susan said, nodding. "She used her position as a file clerk to identify patients who were seriously ill, and then provided their home addresses to a broker, who sold them sham policies. She took a cut."

"Maybe she wanted out. That's why they shot her."

"We don't know that."

"It makes sense though! Anna specifically recalled patient charts from twenty dead patients. Presumably she isn't selling policies to dead people, which means she must have been checking up on—"

"Her past customers," Susan said.

"Exactly. Maybe she felt guilty. Or who knows? Possibly she thought the insurance was legit, but then she started to suspect the truth."

"She had to know giving out patient addresses was wrong."

I nodded. "What she did was illegal. But she thought she was helping people! That fits with everything I've heard about her, and what I knew of her."

Susan regarded me with an eyebrow raised. "You seem rather enthused about this theory. Why?"

"Because it fits! Up until now, nothing has made sense about this crime. Not her death, not the drugs, and certainly not the money. And we must consider Anna's character. I can't believe she was purposefully stealing money from cancer patients. But if she viewed herself as an angel of mercy, providing help to families who needed it—"

"Then she was idealistic and naïve."

I shrugged. "Good people often are."

She turned the key in the ignition and pulled onto the road.

"What's next? Do we go interview more families? Or should we look for information on that insurance company? Maybe—"

"I'll drop you off at home."

"But I can help," I said.

Susan smiled. "You've been a big help already, but I'm not dragging a civilian back to the office. It wouldn't be appropriate, and I have access to databases you don't. Tell you what, though. I'll check in with you when I have news. In the meantime, I need you to do something for me."

"What's that?"

"Keep your lips zipped."

"Okay."

"I'm serious! Whoever these guys are, they're dangerous, and I don't want them spooked."

I pantomimed locking my mouth and throwing away the key, but Susan was preaching to the choir.

I knew what was at stake, and I'd been careful. Sure, I probably should have told Susan about the threatening note, and I would, soon. But not yet, I didn't want her shutting me out when we were so close to the answer.

Susan dropped me off at my condo, but instead of going inside I walked a few blocks down Broadway to get a cup of coffee at Vivace. As happy as I was about our discoveries, something about the case wasn't sitting right in my mind. It was almost as if there was a red flag waving just outside my peripheral vision, trying to tell me something.

For all investigations, be they a murder investigation or the case of who was stealing lunches in the breakroom, the process was the same. Drink coffee. Gather data. Separate fact from fiction. Repeat as necessary.

WHEN I GOT HOME, I fed Milo. Derek wouldn't be over for another three hours, and I was too full of energy to sit around waiting. I sat on the couch and scratched Milo behind the ears.

"I'm going for a walk," I said, giving up on my attempt to relax. Milo didn't want to leave my lap, even when I tried to get up. In the end I had to remove him by unhooking his claws from my pants, one by one. "I'll be back soon," I told him.

The air was brisk, but the thick blanket of clouds kept the temperature well above freezing. And by some miracle, the rain was slacking off. I walked past the Broadway Rite Aid with its gaudy pink and blue marquee, turned right on Olive Way, and headed downhill toward the city center.

How did this 'polite young man with freckles' coordinate with Anna, I wondered? Was he part of a gang, or had he operated alone?

A Metro bus ran a yellow light, causing nearby cars to honk in musical disapproval. The light turned red and a UPS driver waved me forward as I hesitated at the curb. I gave him a wave and crossed the street. The rain started back up, fat drops but not too many of them.

If the murderer came prepared to frame Anna, bringing drugs and a crowbar, that meant they knew she was a problem. And how could they know that? I doubted she'd volunteered the information, especially once she knew how dangerous they were.

Now, if they'd known she was pulling the files of their victims, that might have tipped them off. And to know that, they needed to work in the hospital. Probably right inside the medical records department.

I turned right on first avenue and walked through the Belltown neighborhood. The rain was falling steadily now, and my hair was dripping into my eyes. But I was only a few minutes from the office.

My main problem was that no one I knew at work fit the description given by Josh's late wife.

Names were easy; show me a name and I'd have read it somewhere, in our database or on a time sheet. But faces were trickier. I wished I could ask Jocelyn, she knew just about everyone.

At the hospital, and I walked through the lobby and let my fingers brush against the base of Sister Constance's statue. Jocelyn wasn't working today, she was on her date with Phil, but I had the next best thing: our employee database, which contains photos of every person who works at Holy Heart.

If what Susan said was true, about this scam being new to Seattle, I'd bet whoever this person was they'd been hired within the last year, and they'd come from another hospital system.

A life insurance scam wasn't the kind of thing you could get away with forever, but if they did it well, they could disappear before anyone got suspicious.

I pressed my security badge against the black pad to gain access to the administration building, but I didn't bother flipping on the lights.

Once I reached my office, I pulled up our employee database and ran a report showing all employees, sorted by hire date. I'd need to click on each record to see the photos, one at a time, but if I hurried I could get it done in time to grab a taxi and meet Derek back at my place.

A young polite guy with curly hair and freckles, I said to myself, as I flicked through employee records. Our name badge photos aren't high resolution, so it was slow going. Anytime I ran across a possible fit, I opened the image full-size and scrutinized it.

About an hour later, I reached the end of the list. And I'd found nothing! Well, we had a few employees with freckles, but none of them were particularly young, nor did they bear even a superficial resemblance to the photo of Josh Cutbert's son. I wrote down their names anyway, to pass on to Susan. If she ran into a dead end, it would be another avenue to pursue.

I felt a sweet surge of relief. As eager as I was to find Anna's killer, the idea that I might have hired the person made my skin crawl. And if they weren't one of us, our employees might be safer.

On my way out of the department, I checked my mailbox out of habit. There were a couple interoffice envelopes in there, one contained a recommendation for an employee service award, and the other held a corrected timecard. I tossed the empty yellow envelopes into the white corrugated plastic container we used to send papers back and forth between departments.

Wait. That red flag was waving again, but this time it was right in front of me. Who had access to Holy Heart facilities? And who was in a position to be intimately aware of what was happening in our investigation? And how did the person who had threatened me gotten access to an interoffice envelope? A polite young man with freckles! I hadn't noticed the freckles, but it made sense with that red hair.

It was all in front of me! I pulled out my phone and dialed Susan's number. Her voicemail picked up; that was fine, I'd leave her a message and grab a taxi to the precinct. "Susan. You're not going to believe this. It all makes sense! I know who did it! He's—"

The front door of the HR department slammed shut, and I froze. Was it Susan? I almost called out to her, but how would she have gotten in without a key?

I held my breath and listened. There wasn't any sound, and after a moment I began to wonder if I'd imagined the whole thing. Perhaps a car had backfired outside, I thought.

A dark figure passed through the lobby, moving toward my office with purposeful steps. *Shit*. Our emergency exit was on the other side of the department, and I'd have to walk right past him. But if he was inside my office, I could run out through the lobby.

My heart pounded. *Move!*

I flinched, but my feet didn't move. I'd need to cover a good twenty feet of ground to get through the lobby, and he'd be behind me the whole time. Too dangerous. There was a window in the mailroom, but I'd need to stand on the file cabinet to reach it. Too noisy?

Options. I had options. But none were good. The phone in my hand beeped; I'd run out of time on Susan's voicemail. How loud was that beep? Did he hear it? I peered into the dark hallway and thought again about making a break for it.

Quick footsteps were moving toward me, partially muffled by the carpet. I grabbed something heavy off the mail room counter and ducked behind the copy machine. I was trapped now, and the copier provided only partial cover, but he might pass me by.

I waited, trying to slow the thudding of my heartbeat by the sheer force of my will.

INVOLUNTARY TURNOVER

Where was he? My heartbeat was like a fist punching sheet metal. I steadied my heels against the floor, my body tense like a spring, ready to strike.

He stepped in front of me, close enough for me to touch. There was something small and metallic in his hand, and he started to turn.

I sprang upward, swinging my weapon in a wide arc. The gun swung opposite, the opening of the barrel moving toward my face.

There was a loud crack. Pain. Acrid black smoke burned my eyes, and I fell to the ground.

Darkness.

CHAPTER THIRTY-TWO

"HOLD STILL." DR. CONWAY WAS SHINING a bright light in my eyes, and I was squirming. My eyes hurt, a lot, and the light made it worse.

"How bad is it?" I asked.

"You're going to be fine. You got a face full of toner, and some stippling from the gun fired at close range. My nurse is going to give you another eyewash; we want to get all that nasty chemical out of there."

"God, I feel like I soaked my eyeballs in Sriracha. And I'm hungry. No, thirsty. Is the Starbucks on the corner open?"

"I'll give you an anti-inflammatory," Dr. Conway said.

"Coffee has antioxidants."

"Hush." He took the bright light away.

Mary Cisneros came with an eyewash kit, and her nose wrinkled when she looked at me. I didn't know what stippling was, but it sounded terrible. Would I spend the rest of my life under layers of pancake makeup? I didn't even like regular makeup! It was all too much work.

"You've got tiny burns on your face. Like freckles, except they're black."

"Burns from the discharge of a .38," said a familiar voice. "While that's better than taking an actual bullet to the face, they'll take time to heal."

"Susan?" I was lying back on the exam table while Mary poured something soothing into my eyes.

"Is she going to be okay?"

"I predict a full recovery," Dr. Conway said.

The detective sounded exasperated. "You're damn lucky, Kat. The techs say the bullet hit the copy machine less than two inches from your head. The room is a mess, but there's a white spot where you blocked the toner explosion. And you look like you got the world's worst spray tan."

"And the man who I—"

"Our suspect? He'll live, but we won't be able to question him for a while. Can you fill me in?"

There was a commotion outside the exam room. I sat up in time to see Derek, my sister Dori, and the entire HR team converging on me in a single hysterical mass.

"Oh my God! You're okay." Derek grasped my shoulders and searched my face. I wasn't sure if he was going to hug me or shake me. He hugged me hard enough to make my ribs hurt.

"I'm fine."

"I could kill you!" He seemed torn between fury and tears.

"I'm right here, fella." That was from Susan.

"He may have to get in line." Akiko sat down next to me on the other side of the bed. "Why did you have to get shot at? You know we can't run this place without you." She hugged me, too, and then made room for Dori.

"I love you, and I'm glad you're okay," she said. "I'll take you home whenever you are ready."

"Are you questioning her?" Derek asked the detective. "She's represented."

"Yes, we all represent her." This from Davis, who piped up from the rear of the group.

Erin rolled her eyes. "He's a lawyer you idiot. Let him work."

My head was throbbing from all the noise. "Calm down! All of you. I've had a crazy day, and I don't need any more crazy. The detective is taking my statement. Derek can stay and listen. Dori will take me home. The rest of you, chill. I'm fine. I promise."

"We'll wait over there," Dori said, pointing at a row of empty chairs near the elevators.

Derek listened intently as I told the detective everything. When I got to the part about the pictures left on my car, he gave me a look that said we would talk about this later.

"When did you suspect the courier?" Susan asked.

"Just before I heard him come in. No one in our employee database fit the profile described by Josh, but when I checked my mail, it all clicked.

"James had access to all of our departments, and he was personally involved in shuttling patient back and forth. He was even dating Shelby, our medical records manager. She told me he was moving out-of-state, and I kind of forgot about him."

"If he had access to the patient charts, why was Anna involved?" Derek asked.

Susan nodded. "I've been thinking about that. My best guess is that he got greedy. Instead of reading files as he transported them, hoping he'd find someone vulnerable to scam, he could get a pre-screened list from her."

"I still don't believe Anna knew what she was doing," I said. "She must have been duped."

Susan wouldn't speculate. Instead she suggested that Derek take me home.

Mary bandaged my eyes and Derek drove me home, holding my arm as he guided me into my apartment, and into my bed. Dori followed him and slept on my couch that night. Akiko said she'd handle Angela until I was ready to come back.

I slept and slept. Milo curled himself around my head and purred like a freight train.

JAMES PETRA WASN'T THE COURIER'S real name. Susan's team found a quarter of a million dollars in cash and five different driver's licenses in his modest Northgate apartment. There were warrants for his arrest in three other states, most of them for insurance fraud.

According to the district attorney, James had a pattern of using relationships with women to convince them to assist him in his "business." Sometimes the relationship was romantic, and other times he spun the tale that he was helping desperate people get insurance.

He'd used his relationship with Shelby to keep tabs on the investigation. And when she'd told him I was asking questions, he began following me discreetly. Susan questioned Shelby extensively and determined that she wasn't involved in the crime.

Dr. Elsworthy, one of our surgeons, told me it took three hours to pull the small circles of paper out of James's lacerated scalp, and another six to piece together his shattered skull. The heavy-duty three-hole-punch I'd hit him with was bagged as evidence, but Susan told me I wouldn't face any charges. I'd been lucky to survive.

Maybe I should have felt bad about bashing a man's head in with a piece of office equipment, but I didn't. Whenever a guilty thought tried to push its way into my brain, I thought about Anna Vasquez and her grandkids. Also, the way he'd tried to shoot me in the head to shut me up. Mostly, I tried to put it out of my mind.

Anna's murderer had been caught only because her friends hadn't given up on her. Like most good things in this world, no one person could have done it alone. Bringing that man to justice had been a team effort, and I felt proud to have been a part of it.

I returned to Holy Heart two days after the attack and was the recipient of more hugs than I felt comfortable with. To my relief, after I explained to Sally and Bridget why I'd been keeping them at a distance, they forgave me.

While no definitive proof was found, Susan believed the pharmacy break-in was an attempt to cover up the real cause of the murder. The police think Anna grew suspicious of James, and when she confronted him, he'd killed her. In the end, it was the hard evidence that put him away. The stuff in his apartment, along with the gun. He'd used the same one on me that he'd used in Anna's murder.

The day after Anna's name was officially cleared by the SPD, the entire Vasquez family descended in force on the HR department with a homemade lunch. Angela even stopped by, and spent several minutes in intense conversation with Thomas in the hallway. I don't know what they discussed, but Angela was in a good mood for days.

In the end, Erin got her new copy machine. We finally found that loophole we'd been looking for. If your machine is shot to death, and you've got a police report proving you didn't do it, they'll give you a new one.

HR: 1. Bureaucracy: 0.

As for me, I'm still working on the whole "not being a doormat" thing. Just yesterday, Jocelyn came running into my office looking deadly serious.

"Kat," she said, breathing hard, "Gayle says Marcie won't stop wearing low rider pants. She wants you to come and look at them to get a second opinion on if they're gross.

"Oh, and Angela wants to see you immediately. Something about our wall art? She says we are," Jocelyn held up air quotes, "making a bad impression to our physician candidates. What do you want to do first?"

I glanced out my window. The pale gray clouds were pulling apart, revealing patches of bright blue sky. Derek was approaching our building from the parking lot; he'd offered to take me out to lunch. He saw me looking and waved.

I smiled at Joss and her anxious expression faded away.

"Neither of those things are emergencies. I'll call them both when I get back from lunch, okay?"

"You got it," she said, winking at me before disappearing around the corner, quick like a bunny.

Derek arrived two minutes later, his jacket slung over one arm, "Are you ready to get out of here?"

"Please. We've got another crisis looming, and if I don't leave now, I might never get out."

"Another murder?"

"Worse. Low rider pants, possibly with visible thong."

"Good God. What's wrong with young people these days?"

"It's not a young person. I think she's in her sixties."

"Should I be horrified or impressed?"

"Impressed," I said. "She's sticking it to the man! Refusing to be held down by the corporate machine." I held up a clenched fist in salute.

Derek laughed and shook his head at me. "Are you sure you're in the right profession?"

As we walked through the lobby, I caught sight of Akiko and Jocelyn. They were in the conference room sword fighting with weapons made from wrapping paper tubes.

I smiled at their antics, and looped my arm around Derek's. "No. But even a job like mine has its moments."

WHAT'S NEXT FOR KAT VOYZEY?

Involuntary Turnover was the first book I ever wrote, and it wouldn't exist without the support of some wonderful people. Putting your work out into the world is scary! I'm grateful for those who helped me along the way.

To my husband Patrick: Thanks for encouraging me, supporting me, and being my partner in all things. I love you.

To my editor Nicole: Thanks for the good advice, the boosts to my confidence, and all those missing commas!

To my friends and family: Thanks for helping me believe I could do this. You were right! And it's been so much fun.

More from this Series

For a complete list of books in this series and for the latest Kat Voyzey news, visit **cheribaker.com/kat**

ABOUT THE AUTHOR

Cheri Baker wrote her first novel during a week-long power outage after several trees crashed through the roof of her house. Because sometimes you need an escape from reality!

The lights came back on, and the stories kept on coming. In 2019, after many years in the corporate world, she traded her suits for jeans and became a full-time author.

Today, Cheri is an author of mystery, suspense, and speculative fiction. She lives in Seattle with her husband, and she's working on her next novel. That is, when she's not drinking coffee, watching monster movies, or blogging about what's on her mind. You can learn more about Cheri, her books, and her upcoming projects at: cheribaker.com

Made in United States
Orlando, FL
05 January 2024